"I'M NOT SUPPOSED TO TALK ABOUT IT, BUT MY MOTHER WAS A SPY—A SPY AGAINST THE RUSSIANS."

Kevin rolled his eyes so far into his forehead that I hoped they'd get stuck there. "Oh, please!" he said. "Who do you think you're kidding?"

"Vada," Judy said. "You mean your mother had you *in* jail *in* Russia?" Then Kevin took her arm, and they started down the hallway.

As I stood watching them walk off, I began thinking about something that had nothing to do with my mother or the writing project or even my big fat lies.

It was a really, really weird thought. Well, I mean, I often have weird thoughts, but this was the weirdest of all. I can't stand Kevin Phillips; yet as I watched them walk away, snuggling, I began to wonder: What would it be like to kiss him?

Jeez! I opened my locker and stuck my head in. And had another weird thought.

Would I rather write a really good poem, I wondered, or get a really good kiss?

Point

MY GIRL 2

A Novel by Patricia Hermes
Based on the motion picture screenplay
written by Janet Kovalcik
Based on characters created by Laurice Elehwany

■SCHOLASTIC

Scholastic Children's Books,
Scholastic Publications Ltd,
7-9 Pratt Street, London NW1 0AE, UK

Scholastic Inc.,
555 Broadway, New York, NY 10012-3999, USA

Scholastic Canada Ltd,
123 Newkirk Road, Richmond Hill,
Ontario, Canada L4C 3G5

Ashton Scholastic Pty Ltd,
P O Box 579, Gosford, New South Wales,
Australia

Ashton Scholastic Ltd,
Private Bag 92801, Penrose, Auckland,
New Zealand

First published in the US by POCKET BOOKS, a division of Simon &
Schuster Inc., 1994

First published in the UK by Scholastic Publications Ltd, 1994

ISBN 0 590 55810 2

Printed by Cox & Wyman Ltd, Reading, Berks

10 9 8 7 6 5 4 3 2 1

For Sharon Newman

MY GIRL 2

CHAPTER

I

I remember before I was born. Wadded up like a fur ball in the highly overrated fetal position. Luckily I'm not claustrophic, but on rainy days I still feel a tightness in my left shoulder. So now that my stepmother's pregnant, I understand what the new baby's going through and I'm not jealous at all. Really. Not at all. It's dark in there . . . and crowded . . . and if this baby's anything like me, it can't wait to get out.

I hope it gets out all right. I mean, everybody does—get out, that is—one way or another. Except sometimes something happens when the baby's trying to get out, and the mother dies. That's what happened to my mother when I was born. She had me. Gave me a name—Vada. And then she died. And I never, never got to know her.

Nothing's going to happen to Shelly, my new

stepmom, though. No way. Two times in the same family couldn't happen. I don't believe in coincidences, and besides, I've decided that if you think hard enough and concentrate hard enough, you can make things go the way you want them to. Most of the time. So I'll concentrate real hard, and I won't let anything happen to Shelly. Or the baby.

Thomas J, my best friend—well, he used to be my best friend, but he died, too—he would have understood me when I said that. Other people, like my new friend, Judy, don't quite understand, even though I like Judy a lot. But I still miss Thomas J. I suppose it sounds like I'm morbid and that everybody I hang around with dies, but that's not true. Thomas J just had a terrible accident. But since I'm talking about this death thing, I may as well tell the whole story and get it over with: I live in a funeral home. Really. That's because of what my dad does—he's an undertaker.

But I'm not morbid. Maybe a little worried, though, especially lately. Shelly was getting super fat with the baby, but she couldn't seem to eat anything. Everything made her sick. And Dad was beginning to make *me* sick, he was getting so nervous.

Like today. We were all sitting around the table, eating—or trying to eat—Dad and Shelly and me, when Dad started fussing over Shelly again.

"You didn't finish your meat loaf," he said, frowning down at her plate and then looking up into her face.

"If I eat it, I'll throw up," she answered, almost in

a whisper. She made a little bulgy pout with her mouth, like she was going to throw up right that second.

"Try a little bit?" Dad said. He actually held out the fork, like he was feeding a baby.

"Then I'll just throw up a little bit," Shelly said.

I got up and started to clear the table, or I thought *I'd* throw up. Besides, it was time to help Dad and Arthur set up the front parlor for a funeral.

I bent over Shelly's stomach as I went by. "Baby?" I whispered. "You sure you want to get involved in this?"

The baby didn't answer—obviously—but Shelly whispered, "You're a love, Vada." Then she gave me a sweet smile, even though I could see she was holding back the throw-up.

I got out of there in a hurry.

I went into the front parlor, where we had a dead old lady all set up on a platform with dozens and dozens of flowers around her, and more flowers that kept getting delivered. She must have been very nice, or very rich.

Anyway, it was my job to help set up chairs and stuff. Used to be I couldn't bear to go near the room where we put the dead people, but I've gotten better. I guess you can get used to anything.

I was helping Arthur, and then Dad came in. I was sort of singing along with the song in the background, that song about a fine house.

Arthur was singing, too, and then Dad chimed in.

Arthur has a really nice voice, but Dad . . . ? He

should learn to hum. Or stick with playing his tuba. He belted out the part about some cats, and I shuddered.

He sounded a little bit like a wailing cat himself.

"Hey, Vada," he said, breaking off his song, fortunately. "Try to scrunch those chairs together a little more, okay?"

I rolled my eyes at him. "Dad! I'm trying. They're chairs. They don't scrunch."

"And I guess we set up chairs in the library," Dad went on. "Then we pipe in the sermon like we did for old man Hazelmeyer."

"In that case you'd better fix that speaker," I said. "It makes the minister sound like an astronaut."

The doorbell rang, and Arthur went to answer it.

Arthur is really neat. He's been working with Dad for about forever. Uncle Phil, Dad's brother, used to work with Dad, too, but he left a while ago to go to Los Angeles. He said he needed a change.

I miss him a lot, but I sure can't blame him for needing a change. Working with dead people all the time gets very—deadly or something.

I heard Arthur come back in, and I turned to look. More flowers delivered for the nice—or rich—old lady?

But it wasn't flowers. It was Judy. My new friend Judy.

"Look who I found," Arthur said.

"Hi, Judy," I said.

"Hi," she answered. "Hi, Mr. Sultenfuss."

4

"Hi, come on in!" Dad said, bending over some chairs again, still trying to make them scrunch.

But Judy wasn't coming in. She was just standing at the door with kind of a sick look on her face. I almost laughed. The look reminded me a little bit of how Shelly had looked earlier—as if she was about to throw up.

"Judy," I said. "It's just a corpse!"

"I know that!" she said, sounding kind of snotty.

"Well, that's nothing," I said. "You should be here when they bring in a body that's been dead for a couple of days, when they haven't found it because it was in an apartment where no one came to visit, or floating in the river . . ."

Judy put up one hand like she wanted to stop me, but at the same time I could see she was really interested—everybody's interested in dead bodies —so I went on.

"Anyway," I said, going back to arranging chairs. "Then the body starts turning this weird shade of green, you know? Like watery pea soup. And the arms and legs deteriorate after the body. It looks like a raisin with four fat legs. Anyway, this is why I'm seriously considering cremation."

I bent over to fix one stupid chair that was stuck, then looked up at Judy. But she wasn't in the doorway.

"Judy?" I said. "Judy?"

Arthur gave me a look, half frown, half grin. "I think you lost her on the pea soup, sweetie," he said.

5

"Jeez!" I muttered. "What a chicken."

Now what was I going to do for the rest of the day? Who was I going to hang out with? The room was set up and we were all finished.

Oh, well, she'd be back.

Dad and Arthur and I took one last look around the room. Then Dad and I went back to the living room, in our part of the house in back. I guess I hadn't been totally nice to Judy. I mean, not everybody wants to know all that stuff. But if she's going to be my friend, she may as well know what it's like to live in a funeral home.

Dad and I found Shelly sitting on the couch— fatly.

She was watching TV and laughing at something, and I was relieved to see her looking better.

Dad sat down next to her, picking up some mail that was on the end table and flipping through it.

He looked up at me. "I can't find the card now," he said, "but I got one today. Or yesterday. It was from Uncle Phil in L.A. He said he went body-surfing."

"Uncle Phil?" I said. "I don't know if I can picture Uncle Phil bodysurfing."

Shelly laughed. "I don't know if I want to," she said.

I laughed, too. I mean, I love Uncle Phil. But he's . . . well, like old. Dad's age at least.

"Vada?" Dad said.

He was still looking through the mail, but his voice

6

had suddenly gotten hesitant. He was also deliberately not looking at me.

Uh-oh. Whenever he wants something from me or is worried about my reaction, he gets like that. He looked just the way he did when he told me that he and Shelly were getting married.

I just waited it out. It's the only thing to do.

"Vada," he said again. "I want to ask you a favor. And remember, you can absolutely say no if you want to."

Right.

I saw Shelly shoot him a look. "I thought we decided not to do this," she said.

"I'm just bringing it up for discussion, that's all," Dad said.

Like I wasn't even there!

I folded my arms. "Do what?" I said.

Dad swallowed. "Well," he said. "The thing is, your bedroom is right next to our room, and we thought—if you were willing—we might move you to Gramoo's old room and use your old room for the nursery. We'll be up half the night with the newborn and—"

"You want me to *move?*"

Move out of my room! It's been my room since even before I was born. Dad told me that my mother picked out the color before I was born—pink—and painted the room herself, she was so sure I was going to be a girl!

Nobody said anything.

"You want me to *move?*" I said again.

"Not far," Dad said. "Just down the hall. Gramoo's room is a lot bigger. Plus, you get a view of the neighborhood."

I looked from him to Shelly.

Shelly looked really upset—worried and sad. And mad, too, I thought. Like she hadn't wanted Dad to do this.

But what could I do? They wanted the room. The baby was coming. *Their* baby. Nobody had asked me if I wanted that, either.

I slumped down on the couch "Sure," I said. "Sure. No problem."

CHAPTER

II

*L*ater that night when I was in my room—*my*
room, my own room, the one my mother painted for
me—I leaned my elbows on the windowsill and
looked out at the night.

It was pretty late and very dark, and Dad was out
on the porch playing his tuba softly. I swear, I don't
know how the neighbors put up with it, but so far
nobody's complained, that I know of—nobody, that
is, except for the dogs. A few of them were howling
along now as Dad played one of these weird old songs
that he loves.

But he wasn't playing for me, that was for sure, or
he wouldn't want me to give up my room.

I watched and listened for a while, then saw Shelly
come out on the porch and stand beside him.

He stopped playing, and I saw both of them turn
and look up toward my window.

I backed up. I didn't want them to think I was spying on them, although actually lots of times I have spied on them from there. You can see everything, and voices float up at you. So I wasn't surprised to hear Shelly's words absolutely clearly.

"Harry?" she said. She put a hand on his arm. "Harry, I hate to interrupt you, but I think Vada is upset."

"What do you mean?" Dad said. "She's fine. She'll love her new room."

"Look," Shelly said, leaning against Dad. "We react to every little kick the baby gives. Maybe Vada's trying to tell us something, too."

Duh! Of course I was trying to tell them something: that I want to keep my own room.

I didn't get to hear Dad's answer, though, because they both went back inside then, the dogs still howling away.

But I wasn't surprised next day when Dad invited me to do something he hardly ever invites me to do—go bowling, just him and me. I don't think I've been bowling with him since I was about six, or with hardly anyone else, either, unless you count that one time with Uncle Phil when he got his thumb stuck in a bowling ball and we had to cut the night short. Well, they had to cut the ball off his finger, too.

I guessed Dad must really want that room for the baby.

Anyway, next night there we were in his favorite bowling alley, the one where the jukebox blasts all the time, and the noise of pins being knocked down is so loud that you can hardly hear yourself talk.

Dad had just thrown the first ball and knocked down all the pins except two—two that were pretty far apart. I thought eight out of ten was pretty good, but Dad didn't. Then he had to explain—and explain and explain. You'd think this was a geometry lesson.

"See," he said, holding the ball with both hands and squinting down the alley, "the thing to remember is you must visualize a spare. With a one–ten split, the parabola of the arcing ball must intersect with the apex of the pyramid of pins at precisely . . ."

He pulled his bottom lip under, let his arm drop, swung it back, then flung the ball forward—hurled it forward?

Anyway, it went perfectly down the alley. Perfectly. Stayed right in the center—no gutter ball for him—and sailed right between the pins, leaving both of them standing. They didn't even sway from the breeze.

I did *not* laugh.

But there was no doubt that Dad had things on his mind, things that had nothing to do with bowling. So I figured I'd help him get to the point.

As soon as he turned back to me, I said, "So? What's on your mind?"

"Me?" Dad said innocently. "What makes you think there's something on my mind?"

11

"Look, you're passing up your favorite TV show to go bowling. With me! You've got to have some angle."

Dad just stared at the ball return, searching for my ball, as if it were the most interesting thing he'd seen in a while.

"I don't know," he said. "I just thought it would be nice if the two of us had an evening out, so we could . . . talk."

He found my ball and handed it to me, but I noticed him swallowing hard.

"Shelly's already told me about boys," I said quietly.

"This talk isn't about boys," Dad said. "It's about . . ." He took a deep breath. "Look, I know there are a lot of changes going on, and I'm sorry you're upset about losing your room. But the baby's got to sleep somewhere. Right?"

Right.

I turned to the alley and took my turn. Two throws: one gutter ball, one pin.

Oh, well. Nothing else was going right, either.

I came back and sat down. "It's okay," I said. "Really. It really is. And you know what? You're handling this father-daughter talk very well. I do understand. Really."

Dad stood up, smiled, and gave this huge sigh of relief, as though the whole world had come right again. He wiped off his ball and went to the head of the alley, taking up this really weird crouching stance. "Honey," he said, not turning to me but smiling, I could tell. "That's very mature of you. I'm proud of you. Very, very proud of you."

"Yup," I said, sighing. "Maybe I should move to China. One kid per family. That way you never lose your room."

Dad shot a look at me over his shoulder, then turned back to face the pins.

"Of course," I added. "That may be where they hate girl babies."

Dad made this little nose noise as if he had just exploded, and when he threw the ball, it didn't go anywhere. Instead, it sort of stuck on his hand, dragging him a few feet down the alley.

Uh-oh! He wasn't going to get stuck like Uncle Phil did that time, was he?

But the ball fell off and Dad retrieved it. He came back and plopped down beside me. He held up his hands. "Okay!" he said. "Okay, okay. Keep your room. We'll put the baby out in the yard."

"No! Don't do that!" I said, grinning. "You've got the whole garage."

Dad didn't even smile back. "Sure," he muttered. "Right between the power mower and the weed whacker."

"Now you're talking," I said, and I leaned an arm on his shoulder.

But then, seeing him sitting there looking so very glum, I knew it wasn't fair to tease him this way. I mean, I *did* want my own room. But I knew I'd give it up, too. For the new baby—their baby.

"Dad?" I said. "I'm kidding. You can have the room."

Dad looked up at me. "Seriously?"

I nodded. "Seriously."

And then I had a thought, one I hadn't had since I was a little kid and used to think it all the time: I'd run away, maybe go to Hollywood, live with the Brady Bunch. But I knew that was childish and I wouldn't do it, even if my dad and stepmom were expanding my family without even asking me about it. But I made a promise to myself right then and there: I would never fall in love and would never get married, and I would never, never have a baby. And most of all, if I did get weak in the head and do something dumb and get married and have a baby— two babies—I'd never ask my first baby to give up her room for the new one. Not ever, ever, ever.

Dad got up, picked up his ball, then walked to the line, getting into his bowling crouch.

But then I said something, and Dad swiveled around to me and dropped the ball, practically right on his toe.

Well, it wasn't my fault. All I had said was, "I'm thirteen. Maybe it's about time I had my own apartment."

CHAPTER

III

*T*he following day something happened that made me very worried, worried because although I always realized ‧that getting married and being in love started somewhere, I didn't realize just how early it started. It was bizarre, too. I wasn't going to have any part of it, ever. I had promised myself that just the night before.

This is what happened: the day after that bowling night with Dad, Judy and I had planned to go to the drugstore to get some school supplies. But as usual with Judy, we ended up ignoring the school supplies and hanging around at the cosmetics and makeup counter. Judy began by spraying perfume all over herself. She started with just one wrist, and then she put a different perfume on the other wrist, and then a third behind her ears.

I backed away from her, but I couldn't resist trying one of the perfumes myself. It came in a pretty blue glass bottle that said Eau de Toilette—toilet water.

When I was a kid, I thought that meant water that came out of your toilet, and I couldn't understand why anyone would sell it, much less wear it.

"What do you think?" Judy said, sticking first one wrist under my nose, then the other.

I shrugged. How could you tell? Only a bee could love her now.

"My mother wears this one," she added, waving her right wrist.

"Oh," I said. "It's nice."

"Know what?" Judy said, picking up a different bottle. "I heard my mom talking to a friend, and my mom said that she couldn't have any more kids. I'm glad."

"My mother can't, either," I said. "She's dead. It's Shelly who's pregnant."

"How about this one?" Judy said, turning back to me and waving another bottle under my nose.

I shook my head and looked at the label of the blue bottle I was holding. "I'm leaning toward Passion Flower," I said. "Listen to this: 'It combines the traditional floral scent with the musky aroma of—'"

"Uh-oh!" Judy said, and I heard her suck in her breath.

I looked up at her. "What's with you?" I said. "What are you staring at?"

Then I followed her gaze and saw what she was

staring at—boys. Not just any boys, but *the* boys—
Kevin and the rest, that whole bunch from school
who think they're just so cool.

"It's Kevin Phillips!" Judy whispered. "I don't
want him to see me!"

"*See* you?" I said. "He can smell you from there."

Judy turned back to the counter, frantically grab-
bing for something, anything to keep her head turned
away.

She came up with a pair of sunglasses.

Good idea. I love sunglasses. Much better than
perfume.

I snatched up a pair from the counter, too—a pair
of great big round green glasses.

No way would any boy recognize me in these
things. My own father wouldn't recognize me. But
why didn't Judy want Kevin to see her?

"Oh, no!" Judy whispered, peering over her
glasses. "He's coming over here! Act natural, totally
natural."

Act natural? You don't act natural. You're either
natural or not. Or something.

Anyway, just as Kevin and all of them came right
up to us, Judy whipped off the glasses and flashed
him this toothpaste-commercial smile, not like any
smile I've ever seen her do before. Or like any other
smile I've seen, for that matter, outside television,
anyway.

And she called that natural?

"Hi, Kevin!" Judy said. Super bright.

"Hi," he said. Super cool.

Then he turned to me. "Real cool, Sultenfuss," he said. "You look like a grasshopper."

He laughed really loud, and all his jerky friends laughed, too. And then they all turned and walked away, just like that.

I just made a face at their backs. But when I looked at Judy, I was surprised to see her looking mad, too. How come? He hadn't made fun of *her*.

"What's the matter with you?" I said.

She pinched her lips together tightly. "He likes you," she said.

"Likes me?" I said, frowning. He called me a grasshopper!"

"Boys who like you always always pretend they hate you," she said.

"That's ridiculous!" I said, leaning against the counter. "I suppose," I said, "that also means if they can't stand you, they pretend they're crazy about you?"

Judy shrugged. "I don't know," she said, turning away and plunking down her glasses. "And I don't care. Kevin's a jerk, and I don't like him anymore. He's all yours."

But I saw her watching him through the window as he walked away with his friends, and I thought she looked sad.

"Want to come home with me?" I said, trying to make her feel better. "I'm going to work on my new room. And maybe you could stay to supper? We're moving me, you know, moving my room."

"You got dead bodies?" she said.

I nodded. "Two of them this week."

She shuddered. "No, thanks. Some other time."

"Well, they're not in my *room,* you know," I said. She just shrugged.

I put the glasses back on the counter, and we left the store. We walked to the corner together, then went our own ways.

I had a feeling it wasn't dead bodies she was upset about, though, but boys. Oh, well, what did I know?

I went back home to find Dad and Arthur shuttling books and boxes up and down the hall and taking my bookcases apart. Shelly was standing around helplessly, kind of supervising things, but mostly being in the way.

Watching them, I felt kind of helpless, too. My bed had already been taken apart and was standing up against a wall.

I wondered when they'd begin moving the baby's things into my room.

"Hey, Vada!" Dad said when he saw me. "You have to tell us where things go."

Go? How should I know where they'd go?

Shelly put an arm around me, and I leaned against her—but not too hard. If she ever fell over, we'd never get her on her feet again.

"So, you guys," Arthur said, looking up at Shelly and then at Dad. "Have you thought of any more names for the baby?"

Shelly put both hands on her back and thrust her belly forward, easing the pressure on her back, it looked like. "If it's a girl," she said, "I'm kind of leaning toward the name Esme."

"Esme?" Arthur said. *"Esme?"*

Dad nodded. "I know," he said. "It sounds like a noise your nose makes."

He and Arthur both burst out laughing.

I looked at Shelly and rolled my eyes, but she just smiled. How could she think they were funny? That was absolutely gross.

"What if it's a boy?" Arthur said.

"Oh, Harry junior, of course," Dad said.

A boy! In this house? A baby boy? He'd grow into a big one!

"Dad," I said suddenly. "When a boy likes you, does he pretend that he doesn't like you? And if he pretends he doesn't like you, then how do you ever know if he does like you?"

"What boy likes you?" Dad said, dropping his pliers and turning around and frowning at me.

"It's just a question," I said. "It's not about anybody."

"I think what you're referring to," Shelly said, moving closer to me and putting a hand on my hair, "is men's fear of rejection. Men will do anything to avoid looking weak."

"That's ridiculous," Dad said, picking up his pliers and going to work on my shelves again.

"Is not," Shelly said. She turned to me. "Listen,

Vada, if a guy says he wants to do homework with you, it really means he didn't have the nerve to ask you out on a date. So you get all your books together and pretend to be studying, and the next thing you know, you're ordering pizza and talking about your favorite movie stars."

"So what you're saying is . . ." I frowned at her. "What *are* you saying?"

"It's just that guys don't want to appear overanxious," Dad said. "So if there's a guy you think might like you, let him know you like him so he won't feel he's taking such a risk when he's thinking of asking you out, okay?"

Really? I had to run this one past Judy. Maybe she was right about guys acting as if they hate you if they like you. But how did you deal with all that stuff, anyway? "I'll be back in a minute," I said.

I went downstairs to call Judy, but then I had a thought: I couldn't stand hanging around here watching Dad and Arthur take my room apart. Maybe I'd just go over to Judy's and talk to her in person. Maybe I could even get her to change her mind about staying for supper.

Anyway, it was clear nobody needed me here.

I hopped on my bike and rode to Judy's. I dropped my bike on her front lawn and rang the bell.

It took a minute for her to answer the door, and when she did and saw it was me, she seemed sort of embarrassed. "Hi," she said.

That's all. Not "Come in." Not anything. She just

stood right in the center of the doorway, sort of blocking it so I couldn't see past her.

"Uh," I said. "Hi."

"Hi," she said again. And just kept standing there.

Well, I sure wasn't going to stand on the steps talking about guys and rejection like I was a salesman or something. But I had to say something. "What are you doing tomorrow?" I said. "I thought you might want to go downtown with my dad and me to pick out wallpaper for my new room."

Judy moved farther into the center of the doorway. "I, uh . . . I don't know. I mean . . ."

And then, over her shoulder, I saw what was making her embarrassed. Kevin! Kevin Phillips in Judy's house! Kevin holding up a bottle of milk.

"Hey!" he called. "Is it okay if I drink this?"

Man, was I glad I hadn't started talking about guys and rejection!

"It's okay with me!" I said. "Hi, Kevin!"

He came farther toward the door. "Oh," he said, "if it isn't Vada the Grasshopper Girl."

"Stop it, Kevin!" Judy said.

"I was kidding," he said. "It's a joke. Okay?"

Judy gave me a *look,* and I instantly I knew she was dying for me to go away. But I could also see she felt like she had to explain. "We were just watching TV," she said. "It's a thing about the solar system. You know, it's homework, and we've got that science project coming up and . . ."

I turned away. "Right," I said. "And next thing

you know, you'll be ordering pizza and talking about your favorite movie stars."

I jumped down the steps and onto my bike and headed for home.

Homework! Pizza and movie stars. Judy and Kevin.

So what did I care?

CHAPTER IV

*T*he only thing I cared about then was whether or not Dad and Arthur had put my bed back together in Gramoo's old room, because I was going to bury my head under a pillow and not come out for a week.

Stupid parents. Stupid so-called friends. Stupid babies. Stupid no room of my own.

I threw my bike on the lawn and went upstairs. Things were quiet in the house now, except for some music coming from Dad and Shelly's room. A walk down to the other end of the hall showed that my bed was set up in Gramoo's old room, although it hadn't been made up with sheets and stuff. Right by the door was a box of books, and on top was one of my favorites, a book by a poet that I had learned about from my writing teacher, Mr. Owett: *The Collected Works of Alfred Beidermeyer*. I would get into bed and read, and forget about supposed best friends and stupid boys and stupid babies who make you give up your room.

Man, another favorite writer of mine, Virginia Woolf, she knew you needed a room of your own. How come other grown-ups didn't know that?

But I wanted to take a last look at my old room and the pink walls my mother had painted. I was heading down the hall to look when I realized something kind of sweet: the music I'd been hearing was Shelly softly singing "Baby Love," by the Supremes, with Dad playing along with her on the tuba.

I tiptoed to their door and peeked in.

Shelly was in a big rocking chair, and Dad was sitting by her feet, playing softly and wiggling one foot in time with the music.

Shelly saw me and smiled. "Hi, sweetie," she said. "Come on in. I read an article that says if you sing to the baby, it has a calming influence."

"Assuming the baby's a Supremes fan," I said.

Shelly smiled. "Everybody loves the Supremes. I bet your mom sang to you."

Dad laid his tuba across his lap. "If there was an article about it, I'm sure she did," he said. "She was always reading."

Shelly grinned at me. "It obviously runs in the family." She nodded at the book in my hands. "Is that another new book?" she asked.

I shook my head. "No. An old one. A favorite. *The Collected Works of Alfred Beidermeyer.*"

"Her favorite poet," Dad said, and I thought he sounded kind of proud.

I hadn't even known he noticed what I read.

"Never heard of him," Shelly said. She took a big breath then, and I could see her trying to swallow a burp.

"How about a nice glass of milk?" Dad said, noticing her burp and scrambling to his feet.

A nice glass of milk is Dad's answer to all of Shelly's baby problems.

Shelly nodded, and Dad bent down and put his tuba gently on the floor.

"With taco chips," Shelly added. "So I can dunk."

"What are we hatching here?" Dad said. "Rosemary's baby?"

But he was smiling when he went out.

I came farther into the room and sat down in his place by Shelly's feet.

"Vada," Shelly said, placing a hand on my hair, "you know, when Junior here comes, we're going to need a lot of help from you. I mean, as the big sister you'll be very important in its life."

"Well, sure," I said, "but now that I'll be going into ninth grade, I'll have a whole lot of homework."

I said it because I knew I was being conned—Shelly was just trying to make me feel important. The baby didn't really need *me*. But then I sighed. I mean, Shelly *was* trying. So I added, "But I'll help when I can. You know that. It might even be fun."

Although I wasn't sure of that at all.

Shelly shifted and I looked up at her. From down

there I could hardly see her face because her chest was, well, like enormous.

I must have been staring, because she said, "What?"

"Oh, nothing!" I said. "I mean, really nothing."

But Shelly must have known what I was thinking. "I know," she said. "They're enormous."

I wanted to know something else, but I didn't know how to ask that, either. I mean, how can you ask someone who's already grown up how old she was when she began to have a chest? A chest like I definitely did not have yet.

But Shelly seemed to sense that thought, too, or else she just felt like talking, because she said, "I was a very late developer. They used to call me Shelly Two Backs. All of my friends were already wearing bras except me. Real bras, too, not training bras."

"Why do they call them training bras?" I said. "That's so dumb. It's not like you're learning to ride a bike."

Shelly smiled. "I think it's sort of like preparing you for the rest of your life. Being a woman isn't easy."

"You're telling me," I said.

Shelly shifted around in her chair, sighing a bit.

"Didn't you have a checkup recently?" I said. "Today or yesterday?"

Shelly nodded. "Yup. All systems go. I'm disgustingly normal."

I put my head against her stomach. "Feels pretty noisy to me."

27

Shelly burped. "I had some coleslaw. Don't ask."

I looked around the room. There were about a zillion plants in the room, always were. But now there were more, I could tell. I looked at a particularly tall one over by the window. "Isn't that like the fourth new plant you've gotten this week?" I asked, nodding toward it.

Shelly laughed. "I think I've got the word 'nursery' confused in my mind. I guess I'm just nesting."

She stretched out her legs and suddenly let out a yelp of pain.

"Ouch!" she said, and she began rubbing her leg.

I began rubbing, too. "Is it the sciatica again?" I said, because she had already told me about it.

Shelly nodded, but she could barely breathe with the pain.

"It's nothing to be afraid of," I said, rubbing with her and repeating what she had told me and Dad a zillion times already. "The baby shifts and presses on the sciatic nerve. It's nothing to be afraid of."

"I'm not afraid," Shelly said weakly.

"Good!" I said. I took a deep breath. "Childbirth is a common medical procedure. My mother's case was unusual, really unusual. So don't worry."

Shelly smiled at me, seeming to have gotten her breath back. "I won't worry if you don't worry, okay?" she said.

"Okay," I said back. And inside, I reminded myself again about concentrating, willing everything to be all right. I mean, sciatica is one thing. But that other—we just wouldn't worry about it. It just wouldn't happen.

Then I felt very worried, and guilty, too. I mean, I didn't want the baby in my room, but that didn't mean I didn't want the baby. And I certainly wanted Shelly to be all right.

"Can I get you something?" I said, getting to my feet. "Dad's taking forever. Some milk or pork rinds or . . . How's the pain?"

Shelly laughed. "It's better. But I think I need a nap. Isn't your friend Judy coming for dinner?"

I scrunched up my shoulders, turned, and stared out the window. "She had a previous engagement," I said. I hoped I didn't sound too mad.

If I did, Shelly didn't seem to notice. "In that case," she said, "do you mind if I take a nap?"

I went over to the bed, handed her a little quilt for her lap, and by the time I got to the door, I could see she was nodding off.

I went to my room—no, Gramoo's old room— and flopped down on the bed, staring up at the ceiling.

What a day. My best friend had ditched me for a stupid guy. I'd been evicted from my room. And my stepmother would rather sing Motown than read poetry.

I flopped over on my stomach.

No doubt about it. I was a prime candidate for juvenile delinquency.

CHAPTER

V

*T*he next day in school at least one good thing happened. Mr. Owett, my very favorite teacher in the whole world, started off English class with some poetry.

Mr. Owett is really good-looking for an older person. He reminds me a little of my first writing teacher, Mr. Bixler. Man, did I like him. For a while, a long time ago, I even thought I was in love with Mr. Bixler. I actually wanted to *live* with him, and I still almost die of embarrassment when I remember that I actually *told* him that. But that was before I grew up, and it was also the same time that Thomas J died, so I guess I was allowed to be a little bit of a jerk.

Anyway, I've gotten over that, and I like this new teacher, Mr. Owett. I think he likes me, too, and I know he thinks I'm a good writer—and I am.

Someday I'm going to be a poet, a terrific poet. Well, I already *am* a poet, but someday I'll be a recognized one.

Anyway, that morning Mr. Owett had written out parts of a poem on the blackboard: "Do Not Go Gentle Into That Good Night," by Dylan Thomas. And what a poem that is! Man, if I could write like that . . .

Mr. Owett began class by reading out parts of it from a small volume he held in his hands, his voice very soft, calm, thoughtful. When he got to the part ". . . old age should burn and rave at close of day; Rage, rage against the dying of the light. . . . Do not go gentle into that good night . . ." I thought my heart would stop.

Why? I am definitely not in love with Mr. Owett. Maybe I'm in love with Dylan Thomas?

Right, I answered myself. In love with some old poet?

Or was it something else—just poetry that made my heart feel like that?

Mr. Owett closed the book, and there was a long silence while he looked over the class, and everyone just looked back. Or else, like Judy, they looked away.

Me, I turned to the window, thinking.

"What I want to know," Mr. Owett went on, "is this: I want to know what you think Dylan Thomas is saying here. What does he mean, 'Rage against the dying of the light'?"

There was just one instant of silence, and then

Kevin piped up. "He's mad because they shut off his electricity," he said.

Mr. Cool. Mr. Jerk.

But of course everybody laughed—everybody but me.

Mr. Owett didn't seem upset, though. Instead, he just laughed softly, too. "He's talking about life energy, which in your case, Mr. Phillips, wouldn't cause much of a power shortage."

Again everyone laughed, but I still didn't. I had a thought.

"You know what?" I said, turning back from the window. "I think the poem's really about attitude, about not giving up. It's easy to feel overwhelmed sometimes, but that's when we have to force ourselves to push on. As Alfred Beidermeyer once said, 'To heed the urgent inner voice, embracing destiny, not choice.'"

"Good, Vada!" Mr. Owett said, smiling at me—at the same time that the whole class groaned.

Well, I can't help it if I have a good idea now and then! Jeez!

"All right, class," Mr. Owett went on. "Let's move on to our next assignment. I'm going to give you guys a chance to write."

Again everybody moaned, Kevin louder than anyone.

"Come on, listen up," Mr. Owett said. "I want you to write about someone very special. It should be someone interesting, someone you admire, and someone who's achieved something worth writing about. But it's got to be a stranger. Someone you've never met."

Somebody in the back yelled, "Like President Nixon?"

Mr. Owett shrugged. "Could be. But if you choose someone like Nixon, I want you to investigate the personal side. Did he like to dance? Were his favorite colors red, white, and blue? Play Perry Mason: see what you can come up with."

He waited.

"Okay," he said. "Any ideas?"

Nobody answered.

But I was thinking: someone you've never met, someone who's worth writing about. And for some reason my heart began pounding terribly hard.

"Just remember the two things I said," Mr. Owett went on. "Someone who's achieved something. And someone you've never met."

"I know!" Kevin said. "Elvis. The King."

"I'm doing the one and only Hank Aaron!" some girl yelled from the back.

"Farrah Fawcett!" one of Kevin's gang piped up. "I love to watch that girl run."

There was a long silence again.

And I kept thinking: someone who's achieved something.

But did I dare? And even if I tried, could I find out anything?

No one else in class spoke up.

"You're only going to have a couple weeks, gang," Mr. Owett said, "so start thinking. Next week is spring vacation, and I expect you'll use part of it to do your research. Then in another week it's due to me. Nobody has any ideas?"

More silence. And then Mr. Owett looked at me.

"Vada?" he said, smiling. "What about you? Who have you come up with?"

I took a deep breath and said it. Right out. "My mother," I said.

A couple of people giggled, but mostly there was silence.

I saw Judy glance over at me, a strange look on her face, sort of sad or maybe, I don't know, embarrassed? Did she think I was weird to say that?

Anyway, weird or not, that's what I wanted to do.

Mr. Owett kept looking at me, nodding as though he was thinking. Then after a minute he turned away and went on to someone else.

But when the bell rang and everyone was pushing their way out, he took me aside at the door.

"You know, Vada," he said, "I've been thinking something. Lately I've been rereading Virginia Woolf, and I think she'd be a natural for you. She led a fascinating life and—"

"I'll stick with my mom," I said. "I bet I'll hardly know where to begin once I start. She led a fascinating life, too."

Mr. Owett grinned. "I'm sure she did," he said, and he turned away, juggling a pile of books. "See you next class."

I made my way out into the hall, with Kevin and

Judy right on my heels. They'd probably been listening to every word.

"Jerk!" Kevin said, leaning over my shoulder. "He was giving you an easy out! So you didn't have to write about your mother!"

"So?" I said, turning to face him and Judy. "I want to write about her."

"You're crazy!" Kevin said. "What was her big achievement? Did she invent gravity?"

I made a face at him. "Nobody *invented* gravity. It just exists."

"Then what did she do?" Judy said, hooking her arm through Kevin's.

They were both looking at me, little smiles on their faces, like they were silently laughing at me.

What did she do? She was a great actress, Dad said.

But that wasn't the kind of achievement Mr. Owett meant, was it? I mean, nobody else would think so. Kevin and Judy wouldn't think so. I wasn't even sure I thought so. But I was sure of this: I was going to write about her.

But I couldn't stand the looks on their faces, and I blurted out something—something stupid. "Well," I said, trying to think and talk at the same time, "I'm not supposed to talk about it, but since I'm going to write about it, I might as well tell you. She was a spy, a spy against the Russians."

Kevin rolled his eyes so far into his forehead that I hoped they'd get stuck there.

"Oh, please!" he said. "Who do you think you're kidding? And where did she spy on the Russians from—here in Pennsylvania, I'll bet."

"No!" I said, wrinkling up my face at him. *"Not* here in Pennsylvania. She went to Russia with her acting troupe and got a lot of highly sensitive secret plans sent back. And then, just when she was about to come home, they caught her and killed her."

Kevin laughed right out loud. "All right, big shot," he said. "So when did she have you—between all her acting and spying and being caught?"

"That's simple!" I said. "She was pregnant with me when she went to Russia, but she didn't know it, and when the Russians found out, they waited to shoot her because you're not allowed to kill pregnant women, not anywhere in the world."

Although I knew by now from studying the Holocaust that that surely wasn't true.

Kevin and Judy looked at each other, and they both shook their heads.

"So your mother had you *in* jail *in* Russia?" Judy said.

I took a deep breath. "Well, actually," I said, "I was born in Siberia, and then they shot her and sent me home to my dad."

I was getting in deeper and deeper. Could anyone actually find out if this was true or not?

Kevin took Judy's arm. "Vada," he said, turning away and speaking to me over his shoulder. "That is so much bull. I mean, *so much!"*

He hugged Judy to him. "Come on, Judy," he said, and they started away down the hall.

"Ask anyone!" I yelled after them. "Ask my dad."

But they didn't hear. Not because I didn't yell loud enough, but because they were already snuggling up to each other like nobody else was around at all, like they were in a car or a movie theater or something.

Well, I thought, it *could* be true.

But as I stood there watching them walk off, I began thinking about something else completely, something that had nothing to do with my mother or this writing project or even my big fat lies. It was a really, really weird thought. Well, I mean, I often have weird thoughts, but this was the weirdest of all. I can't stand Kevin Phillips, yet as I watched them walk away snuggling, I began wondering: what would it be like to kiss him?

Jeez! I opened my locker and stuck my head in. And had another weird thought. Would I rather write a really good poem, I wondered, or get a really good kiss?

I stood there for so long I was almost late for next bell, and still I hadn't made up my mind. My very weird mind.

CHAPTER
VI

After school next day—a day when Judy acted like I didn't even exist and she and Kevin were constantly snuggling—Dad and Shelly and I went to the hardware store to pick out wallpaper for my room.

I had told Dad about my project for writing class—to find out about my mother. But I sure didn't tell him about the lies I had made up for Judy and Kevin. I just told him I wanted to find out everything I could, all the stuff he'd never told me. That was the real, honest truth, but no matter what I asked him, he didn't seem to know, or else remember.

Man! I sure would remember everything about someone I was married to! Or maybe his brain was beginning to go, like Gramoo's did before she died?

But I figured it was more like he didn't want to remember. *That* I couldn't understand at all.

"Okay, Dad," I said, trying once more as we went into the hardware store. "I know my mother's favorite color was pink and she ate peanut butter and banana sandwiches for breakfast, but that's not what I call hard facts."

Dad laughed and turned to Shelly. "I told you about the pumpkin, didn't I?"

"No," Shelly said.

I smiled. This was one story I knew, and I loved it.

"Well," Dad said, leaning against the counter where the wallpaper books and rolls of wallpaper were stacked. "I bought her this huge pumpkin for Halloween, and she couldn't bear to carve it up, so she saved it for weeks, and it ended up under the Christmas tree and—"

"And," I interrupted, "on Christmas Eve there was this sickening stench throughout the entire house and—"

"Oh, no!" Shelly said.

"And," Dad went on, "when I picked it up, it sort of exploded and liquefied at the same time."

Shelly burst out laughing.

"Well," Dad said, "it was funny, but it wasn't, too. It soaked clear through Gramoo's Oriental rug and—"

"And there's still a big spot on the floor!" I said.

Shelly just shook her head and started rummaging through the rolls of paper. "I can just picture it!" she said. "There must have been an awful stink. And mess."

She picked up a roll of paper, put it down, picked up another, held her head to one side, considering it.

I picked some up, too, but couldn't find any I liked. What I really wanted was something dramatic, like silver or red, but could I bear to change from pink? My mother's favorite color?

"Dad," I said, looking up at him, "isn't there anything else you remember? How did you propose? Was it romantic?"

"We need wallpaper paste," Dad said. "Propose? I just blurted it out over a root beer float."

"A root beer float," Shelly murmured. "Now, that sounds good."

"Dad!" I said, impatient. "Did she mention any contest she won? She was an actress! She must have had awards. She was so talented . . ."

Dad put a hand on my head gently. "Honey," he said, "I wish I could help, but your mom and I—we had kind of a whirlwind courtship. She came to town with this traveling theater group. I proposed on our second date. Two weeks later we were married. And almost nine months later you were here . . . and she was gone."

I swallowed hard. That was the part that always used to worry me. Maybe still did. That my mother died because of me.

"But," I said, "didn't she—"

"Vada!" Dad said. "I don't know any more. She didn't have any brothers or sisters. Her parents had passed on years earlier, when she was very young.

And the rest . . . Well, I was sort of in a state of shock."

I took a deep breath and shoved aside some rolls of paper. Underneath was a roll of black—plain black.

Now, that would be dramatic! And ugly.

"Was it a nice funeral?" I asked quietly.

"Oh, yes," Dad said. "A lovely funeral. The Grenaldi brothers did a beautiful job. Lots of pink roses. Here!"

He picked up a roll of paper that was lying right in front of me—all flowers but disgusting ones, gaudy ones.

"What about this?" he said. "What about flowered paper for your room?"

And no information about my mother.

"What about this?" I said angrily. I held up the black wallpaper.

I saw him and Shelly exchange looks.

I left them there and went home by myself. They could pick out anything they wanted. This wasn't really my own room, anyway.

I was sitting on the porch when Dad dropped Shelly off, and I watched her lumber up the walk to the steps.

I jumped down to help her, to take her arm.

She had gotten really huge.

"Where's Dad going?" I asked.

"To the morgue," she answered.

I helped lower her into a porch chair.

"Thanks, sweetie," she said. "Want to do something else for me?"

"Sure," I said.

She nodded to her huge old motor home, which she used to drive all the time. Now it was parked by the curb. "I have some new plants in there," she said. "Want to carry them in?"

I just grinned at her. *"More* plants?" I said.

She nodded. "I told you—I've got the word 'nursery' confused in my mind."

I went down and retrieved the plants and carried them into the house, then came back to sit on a chair beside her.

She looked awfully tired.

"Can I get you something?" I said. "You know, pork rinds or milk and taco chips?"

She grinned at me. "Actually," she said, "I'd like to see the spot your mother's pumpkin made."

"Would you?" I said. "Sure!" I helped her up out of the chair.

We went to the far corner of the living room where we always put the Christmas tree, and I bent down and turned back the carpet.

There it was—a dark, dark stain on the wood floor.

I smiled, looking at it. "Know what?" I said. "I used to come down here and sleep on this spot when I was little. Weird, huh?"

I knelt down and put one finger on the spot, the way I used to do, as if I could feel my mother here.

I sighed. "Know what?" I said, looking up at her. "My report's going to be a disaster. Everything I know about my mom fits in a little box!"

"A box?" Shelly said.

I nodded. "A box."

"A box you have?" she said.

"Yup. Want to see it?"

Shelly smiled. "I'd be honored," she said, and she sounded as if she meant it.

Together we went up the stairs—slowly, because going upstairs with Shelly was a little like going upstairs with an elephant. But when I got her settled on my bed, she seemed pretty comfortable.

I went to the dresser and took out my mother's old tin candy box, then brought it back to the bed, where I sat down beside Shelly.

I opened the box and began taking things out— my baby book, which I handed to Shelly, then some theater programs from the Extraordinary Traveling Theater Company, my mother's passport, some pictures and odd bits of paper, and a paper bag with a date on it—all the things I had treasured over the years.

"Oh, what a sweet baby book!" Shelly said, opening the book.

"It's only filled out to page two," I said. "But listen to this."

I leaned over her shoulder and read aloud. " 'Eight pounds, four ounces, twenty-one inches long.' " I shook my head. "Dad has the worst penmanship."

I took the book back, then handed Shelly something else. "It's a receipt for vitamins," I said. "I always wondered why she put this in here."

Shelly smiled. "When you're pregnant, everything has meaning. It's nice that she saved it. And look at this!"

She had picked up my mother's passport and was studying her picture. Quietly she read aloud, "'Margaret Ann Muldovan. Born: Los Angeles, California, February 7, 1936.'"

She looked up at me. "She was lovely. And what a beautiful name. And face."

I nodded. "Know what Dad said once? He said that when she was onstage, she held the audience in the palm of her hand."

"Looking at her, I can see why," Shelly said. She studied the picture again. "Margaret Ann Muldovan," she repeated softly.

"Margaret's my middle name," I said, "but hardly anybody knows that. And nobody called my mother Margaret. Dad said everybody in Los Angeles called her Maggie. Have you ever been to Los Angeles, Shelly?"

"No," Shelly said, leaning back against my pillow and looking up at the ceiling. "I've always wanted to, though. They say it never rains and you can barbecue on Christmas day. And instead of riding a bicycle, you just surf over to your friend's house. I don't think there's anything more romantic than a sunset with palm trees. And the place is crawling with celebrities." She laughed and sat up. "The closest I came to celebrities is this: I know somebody who saw Walter Matthau picking up his dry cleaning."

I laughed. "Wow! But is that why Uncle Phil moved there? Celebrities?"

Shelly shook her head. "I just think Uncle Phil needed a change, a little adventure."

I nodded, and we turned again to the things in the box—more pictures of my mom, one that I had found in a box in the garage with Thomas J one day, one with her standing in a school hallway, with a huge Wilson High School banner strung across the wall behind her. And the small paper bag that has always puzzled me, the one with a date written on it: December 8, 1958.

Shelly fingered it. "What's this?" she said.

I twisted my hair around my finger. "I don't know. Dad doesn't, either."

Shelly took my hand away from my hair. "You shouldn't do that, honey, it'll give you split ends. But the paper must mean something. She was obviously very sentimental."

I nodded. "Very. But you know what? I wonder why she had a passport but it's all blank. Did you notice that? She never went anywhere. Well, not out of the country."

"You've got to be prepared," Shelly said. "I've always wanted to go to Italy, so you know what I did? I just went and got a passport, hoping that one day opportunity might strike."

"And did it?" I asked, smiling.

Shelly smiled back. "When it does," she answered,

leaning in close to me and whispering, like we had a secret, "I'll have my passport."

I laughed. "Well," I said, "I'm definitely traveling someday."

Shelly tipped her head to one side and looked at me—a long, long look. "Someday?" she said.

I nodded.

"Why not now?" she said.

"What do you mean?"

"Well," she answered slowly. "I think you're ready for a little adventure yourself. You have spring vacation next week, don't you?"

I nodded.

"So," she said. "How would you like to do something adventurous? Maybe . . . oh, I don't know, maybe go to L.A. Maybe go to L.A. and visit your uncle Phil?"

I just stared at her. She had to be kidding.

But she didn't look like she was joking.

"You could research that paper on your mom," she went on.

I could. Oh, yes, I could!

"Do you mean it?" I asked.

She nodded. "I mean it."

"But what about you and the baby?" I said. "You need me."

"I do need you, sweetie," she answered. "But I'm not going to have the baby for another six weeks or so. You'll get back in plenty of time."

It would be great. It would be so great!

But I shook my head. I'd love to. But no way.

"Dad'll never go for it," I said. "I know him." And I did know him, too, had known him for a lot longer than Shelly had. No way would he let me out of his sight.

Shelly lifted herself off the bed, and I gave her a hand. "You leave your father to me," she said.

CHAPTER
VII

One week later I was at the airport on my way to Los Angeles. I. Was on my way. To Los Angeles.

Of course, it wasn't as easy as it sounds. First there was a war in the house, a major war.

I was in on some of it, and some of it I just overheard. But to say that Dad wasn't happy wouldn't come anywhere near to saying it.

The first thing I heard was the day after Shelly and I had been to the travel agent—the day after we *snuck off* to the travel agent. She and Dad were having a full-blown fight, the first I had ever heard them have.

I was in my room, and they were downstairs, and I couldn't help overhearing, although I have to admit I tiptoed down the stairs after a while to eavesdrop better. I mean, a lot was riding on that conversation.

Shelly was in the hall, and Dad was partway up the

stairs, but he had turned to face her, so he didn't notice me on the steps above him.

"But you should encourage her to spread her wings!" Shelly yelled.

"She can spread her wings right here in Pennsylvania!" Dad yelled back. "You don't send a *child* to Los Angeles. She'll come back with her ears pierced and her legs shaved and goodness knows what else."

"She's not a *child,*" Shelly said, and this time her voice was quieter, but it was like she was speaking between clenched teeth. "She's a young woman on the brink of—"

"Disaster!" Dad answered back. "Disaster, that's what. Disaster lurks behind every . . . every palm tree!

"You're being narrow-minded," Shelly answered back. "Narrow-minded and—"

"Look!" Dad interrupted, in a tone of voice I recognized and didn't like, that calm, this-is-the-end-of-the-conversation voice. "Maybe when she's a little older," he said quietly, "I will be willing to reconsider."

I knew it was time to speak up. Now or never. Face the lion in his den.

I came down a few more steps. "Dad?" I said.

"Oh, Vada!" Dad said sweetly, turning to me. "We were just . . ."

"Having a fight," I said. "About me. Wouldn't you like my opinion?"

"Uh," Dad said. He looked at Shelly, then at me. "Well, uh, of course we would," he said.

Although I knew absolutely that what he really meant was, of course we wouldn't.

"Okay," I said. "Then I think this: I think that if I'm old enough to accept a new baby, and if I'm old enough to accept a new room, then I'm old enough to go to California."

Dad laughed and shook his head, giving me the kind of smile you give to a kindergarten kid who's being stubborn. "Now, I know it's fun to think about these things," he said. "But, no."

I snuck a look at Shelly, who was staring at her fingernails like they were something brand-new she had never seen before. Had she already told him about the ticket? I hadn't heard her say anything, and I was pretty sure from the way the conversation was going that she hadn't mentioned it.

So it was up to me.

I took a deep breath. "I already bought the ticket," I said.

"You what?" Dad said. He collapsed on the step below me, and I mean, *collapsed,* like a balloon that has just lost all its air.

"I used my own money," I said fast, knowing I had to get it all out before he could start answering back and saying no, just plain no! "I did," I said. "And I got a great deal. It's a Q-forty-seven-NR five-day fare, which means I have to change planes in Dallas and stay over a Saturday in L.A., and there's no exchanges or refunds, so if you don't let me go, I'll have wasted my entire life savings."

"No!" Dad said. "No! It's against the law to sell airline tickets to a minor and—"

I looked over at Shelly again, and now she was looking up from her fingernails. I could tell she was fighting back a smile, and I could also tell that she was about to lose the fight.

"Aha!" Dad said, whirling to face her. "You! Don't tell me you aided and abetted this little scheme."

At this point I tiptoed past them both, then went into the room where the pumpkin spot was. I crouched down over it, but I kept listening to their argument.

"Well," Shelly answered calmly, "Vada needed me. The airline required the signature of an adult, and—"

"And they forgot to ask for one who wasn't having hormone surges!" Dad answered.

Even from in there, I could hear Shelly expel her breath like she was about to scream. But all she said was "Oh, Harry, it's only for five days."

"Five days! Aren't we going a little overboard for a simple school assignment?"

"It's not just an assignment. It's . . . I think maybe all this is happening for a reason."

"All what?" Dad snapped. "What reason?"

"Phil moving to L.A.," Shelly answered. "The baby. Vada's report. Maybe these are signs. Signs that it's time for Vada to take this trip."

"Signs!" Dad moaned, but his voice was much

softer, and I just bet he was shaking his head. Defeat. He was defeated, I could tell.

I stood up, ready to go back upstairs, because I could tell it was all right to start packing now.

But Dad wasn't quite finished fighting back yet. I was just at the door when he gave his last shot, and even I had to laugh. He was stomping up the stairs, yelling, "Let me get the Loch Ness Monster on the phone! You two have a lot to talk about. She's not going, and that's final!"

But that was a whole week ago, and I *was* going. Dad and I were at the airport, having left Shelly home to rest. But Dad was still fussing.

"Now, listen," he said as he walked me to the ramp for the plane. "Remember, don't talk to anyone. If a nun sits next to you, don't even talk to her."

I nodded. "No nuns," I said. "Got it."

"And no boys!" Dad said. "Promise me. Those L.A. people are all corrupt. You'll end up pregnant and on drugs. Don't come running to me when you wake up in the city morgue with a tag on your toe, having been beaten to an unrecognizable pulp by some surfer. And don't make eye contact. It communicates vulnerability."

I just shook my head. My dad is definitely weird. You'd think I was going off on an undercover trip with a bunch of drug lords. "What does 'communicate vulnerability' mean?" I said.

He took a deep breath and moved closer to me. "It means," he said, "I'm a paranoid nitwit who's never let his baby girl out of his sight for the simple reason that he's a paranoid nitwit. So why don't you just say, 'Oh, Daaad!' and get on the stupid plane already?"

I grinned at him. Then I turned, put down my bag, and gave him a big hug. "I'm going to miss you," I said to him.

Dad hugged me back. "Thanks," he said. "I need to know that."

We were right at my gate, and they were announcing the final boarding call for my flight.

I gave Dad another quick kiss. And then, because I could see he needed something else, I added, "I'll be back in a hundred and thirty-seven hours."

He grinned at me, and I went through the doorway where they collected my ticket and checked my boarding pass, and I was on my way.

On my way!

But Dad wasn't finished yet. Behind me I could hear him. "Remember to have fun!" he yelled. "But not too much."

Are all fathers that weird?

On the plane, I checked out all sorts of stuff—my earphones, the magazines—and then lunch was served. The attendant said it was Salisbury steak and potatoes, but I don't think so. I think that maybe they had some dogs traveling in the baggage compartment and they accidentally mixed up the people food with the dog food. Anyway, lunch was grim, and even though I tried mixing the salad dressing with the potatoes, it didn't help. It was too totally gross.

After that I opened my backpack and took out the list Shelly had made up for me: a credit card number for calling home and the name of the person who would be meeting me at the airport—a friend of Phil's named Nick, who would be holding up a sign with my name on it. Then I took out the other things, my mother's things: her pictures, the paper bag with the date, the passport.

I looked at how blank the passport was, yet there was a whole world outside of Madison, Pennsylvania. I sure didn't want my passport to be blank—when I finally got a passport, that is.

But then, sitting there looking out the window, for the first time I started being a little bit nervous. I mean, my airport back in Pennsylvania was crowded and sort of scary and confusing. But the pictures I had seen of the L.A. airport were *really* scary.

Well, maybe not scary. But definitely confusing.

And would I know who Nick was? How would I find him if the airport was as crowded as I'd pictured it, even if he did have a sign? And what if he forgot or something?

Well, I did have Uncle Phil's number.

I sighed and almost laughed at myself. If my dad could have read my thoughts, I knew exactly what he'd have said: I told you so.

CHAPTER

VIII

*F*rom the moment I got off the plane till the moment I got to Uncle Phil's house—well, it wasn't even Uncle Phil's house, but that comes later—things were crazy. I mean, crazy.

First, Nick wasn't a man at all. He was a boy! A guy. A guy about my age. Definitely good-looking and definitely knew it. Not like in the way Kevin Phillips knows it, but in that "I'm cool" kind of way that some guys just have—and like he was doing me a big favor just by being there.

By the time he finally met me and finally snagged my bag for me and sent away some bald guy who was trying to give me flowers and grabbed us a cab right out from under the nose of some lady who was about to get in it with her fancy luggage—by then my head was spinning.

I had never seen so many people in one place in my

life. In fact, I don't think as many people live in the entire state of Pennsylvania as were at that airport. And then, once we got out of the airport in the taxi and I could see things, I couldn't believe it. Palm trees! I'd never seen palm trees before, not in real life, anyway. I mean, outside TV or movies. They're huge, towering up to the sky, but some of them are kind of bald-looking, with raggedy edges. And then, as we drove farther from the airport, we went through this place with fancy houses that were practically mansions. Really! Did Uncle Phil live in one of those? But he couldn't, not unless he had won the lottery or something since I had seen him last.

The whole way Nick hardly said anything. Everything about him showed that he'd rather have been anywhere but with me, and I wondered how he'd gotten hooked into this. Probably Uncle Phil had bribed him or something. When he *did* speak—once —it was so big-deal, like telling me how dumb I was for starting to take the flowers from the man at the airport.

But the guy had said they were a gift for me!

So as we rode, we each stared out our own windows, and after a while the cab got out of the fancy areas and into neighborhoods that weren't so fancy, and I felt more comfortable, yet I had to admit I was a little disappointed. But I was surprised at the place where the cab did finally pull up and stop. It wasn't a house at all, but a garage—Budapest Auto Repair, it said out front.

Uncle Phil's place? Wouldn't surprise me. He's good with cars. But he hadn't told us about that.

Nick paid the cabbie and went in through the front door of the garage, and I followed.

It looked just like I would have expected a car repair place to look—a bunch of cars, a bunch of men working on cars, an oily floor, and the smell of gas and oil. It was also noisy, with people talking and phones ringing, and music playing—but fancy music, not rock music or the kind of music I like. Old people music.

Then, over to the side, I saw him, saw Uncle Phil. He was talking to a guy just getting into his car— talking car talk, the way he loves to. He said something about ball joints and Malibu and parts and labor, and then he thumped the hood of the car as the guy backed out.

And as he turned to wave to the guy, that's when he saw me. He saw me and rushed over to me, throwing both arms around me and hugging me, lifting me right off the floor.

Then he gently set me down, held me away, and looked at me. "Vada!" he said. "Boy, you're a sight! How's the family?"

He looked at Nick, who was standing beside me. "Did Nick take good care of you?" he asked.

"The family's great," I answered. "And Nick was very . . . polite." I made a guess. "Worth the entire five dollars," I added.

Uncle Phil winked at Nick, reached into his pocket, and took out his wallet, then handed Nick a bill.

Nick grinned. "Thanks," he said.

Suddenly a voice bellowed out of nowhere. A woman's voice. Loud! "Give. It. Back!"

We all turned and looked.

There, at the door to a small room that looked like an office, was this woman—this really beautiful woman. She was holding a clipboard in one hand and the phone in the other. She was dressed in a work smock and heavy work shoes, but she could have worn anything and she'd still have been beautiful. Her hair was sort of reddish, sort of blond, thick and curly, and her eyes were huge. Wow!

Nick and Uncle Phil both eyed her, Nick seeming a bit worried, Uncle Phil looking amused.

"We made a business deal," Nick said to her.

"Whatever happened to a good old-fashioned favor?" the woman said.

Nick took a deep breath. He looked at Uncle Phil, and Phil shrugged.

"It's cool," Nick said, and he handed back the money.

"Irving!" the woman bellowed, and I jumped and looked around, searching for Irving, then realized she was speaking to whoever was on the other end of the phone. "Irving, the timing chain is either here or it's not here, and from what I can see, it's not here. Now, do you want to come down here and explain to my customers that we can't reassemble their cars because the parts aren't all here? I have a hard enough time keeping my weight down so I don't need this blubber from you. Are we clear?"

There was a pause, and then she said, "Thank you, Irving. Yes, yes, I love you, too."

Then she plopped the phone down and came across the room to me, both arms outstretched, her manner totally changed—soft and calm and no yelling at all.

She took my face between both hands. "You must be Vada!" she said. Her voice was almost musical and as beautiful as she was. "Oh, what a face!" she said, looking from me to Phil and then back to me again. "If I had a face like that, I wouldn't have to yell so much. I'm Rose, Rose Zigmund. I'm Nick's mother, among other things."

"Nick's *mother?*" I blurted out.

I don't know why I was so surprised, except that she was so beautiful—and so young.

She laughed. "What did you think, he was raised by a pack of wolves? Don't be misled by the haircut."

"Mo-om!" Nick said, his neck and face getting deep red.

I grinned at him.

It was fun to see him get some of it back.

Uncle Phil came and put his arm around Rose. "Who knew that when I got a job with the finest foreign-car repair shop in L.A.," he said, "I'd also meet the light of my life!"

Rose grinned at me and shook her head. "He only left out a couple of steps. Now, listen." She turned to Uncle Phil. "I have to get some bills out. You help Vada get settled, why don't you?"

She turned and went back into her office, and Phil opened a door next to the office that revealed a steep stairway.

Up there? Above the garage? Was I going to stay here?

Uncle Phil must have known what I was thinking because he said, "Come on, sweetie," and he pulled me along after him. "Expect the unexpected."

Upstairs, the apartment was small but bright with sunshine, and very pretty—bright curtains and bowls of flowers and a bunch of small prints on the walls, all clustered together like in an art gallery.

I looked around. I liked it. A lot. But who lived here? It sure didn't look like Uncle Phil's kind of apartment. His was more apt to have dust and car parts and movie magazines.

"Here," said Phil, opening a closet door. "You can put your stuff in here. Luckily, the couch is very comfortable, I can tell you that from personal experience."

I frowned at him. "Are you and Rose . . . engaged or married or something?"

Phil was shaking his head, hard. "Oh, no!" he said. "We're dating, though. Seriously dating. Marriage is a very big step and not something to enter into lightly. I just want to make sure this is totally the right thing before . . ."

I just laughed, laughed hard, and Uncle Phil stopped and frowned at me. I know him. I've known him a long time. He's been a bachelor forever. "It sounds," I said, mimicking what I'd heard Dad say a million times, "as if you have a fear of commitment, Uncle Phil."

"That's ridiculous!" he said. "I'm . . . very committed."

Uncle Phil looked at me, this serious look, like he was about to launch into a lecture.

I just rolled my eyes.

But then, it was their business, not mine. Mine was to find out what I could about my mother, and I had just five days to do it in.

Later, after I was settled, Rose came up from the garage and prepared a nice dinner, all the while talking to me and asking me questions—but nice ones, not the kind of prodding stuff that some grown-ups do, like they're trying to get inside your soul.

So I didn't mind at all telling her what I was doing and why. And when we sat down to dinner, I told them all—Uncle Phil and Nick, too—about my class assignment and how I had chosen my mother. "Instead of Virginia Woolf," I said proudly.

"Any idea what your mother's biggest achievement was?" Rose asked. She smiled at me.

I smiled and looked down at my lap.

"I'm not really sure," I said, looking back up at her. "My dad's words were 'We had a brief but intensely fulfilling relationship,' and she's remained a 'woman of mystery' to this day."

"And you're going to solve the mystery," Nick said.

I glanced over at him. It wasn't exactly sarcastic,

the way he said it, but it wasn't exactly friendly-sounding, either.

"Yes!" I said, knowing it came out kind of defensive-sounding. "I am. I've got it all figured out. I know she went to Wilson High School. First thing tomorrow I'm going there and getting a copy of her yearbook. Yearbooks tell everything, like the names of everybody she was in clubs with. That way I'll find out who her friends were and look them up and—"

I broke off, looking at Uncle Phil. Was this really going to work? Or did this sound as dumb to them as it was beginning to sound to me?

But Uncle Phil was grinning at me. "And then you'll be all set!" he said.

"Sounds like you're very organized," Rose said.

I nodded and sighed. "I hope so. I have to be. I only have five days. So just point me in the right direction, or maybe give me a map . . ."

"I'll do better than that," Uncle Phil said. "I'll send you with your own personal guide."

He looked across the table at Nick.

"Me?" Nick said, and he sounded alarmed. *"Me?"*

"I'd consider it a personal favor," Uncle Phil said, but he winked.

Money. I'd have bet anything.

"I'd consider it a personal *order,"* Rose said.

I looked from one to the other. I wasn't sure how I felt about the favor-order. In a way I was relieved. L.A. was bigger than I'd ever imagined, and I felt a little nervous about going out and finding my way on my own. Yet, being with Nick all day while I looked up my mother's history wasn't something I was exactly looking forward to, either.

But for just one day, I'd see how it went. I could put up with him for one day.

At least that's what I thought, until I overheard something—or rather, saw and overheard something—I wasn't meant to see and hear.

Rose had gone back down to her office, and Nick and Phil were doing dishes. I was standing by the front window overlooking the city, twisting my favorite ring—my mood ring that always reminds me of Thomas J—twisting it around my finger and staring out at the night.

Jeez, it was huge out there—huge buildings and hills and palm trees and the sky that seemed to stretch away into a mist of clouds and haze as the stars came out over the mountains.

It was dark in the room, with just a bit of light coming from the kitchen, where Nick and Phil were making noise with pots and dishes and talking quietly—quietly, but I heard my name. I couldn't resist.

I tiptoed across the room toward the kitchen and pressed myself into a little space between the doorway and the refrigerator, which jutted out into the room. That's when I saw Uncle Phil slip something in Nick's pocket.

"What?" Nick said. "What's that?"

"Ten bucks," Uncle Phil answered quietly. "Just a

little something for the minibike fund. I know you're not exactly crazy about taking Vada around tomorrow."

I backed up, all the way back to the window.

Nick wasn't crazy about taking *me* around! Jeez!

Well, I'd just show him how crazy I was about being stuck with *him!*

_____ *CHAPTER*

IX

Which is exactly what I did the next day, though I had to be careful, because he knew his way around and I didn't.

I had the address of Wilson High School from an old play program—1759 West Washington Boulevard, corner of Seventeenth—but L.A. is not like any city I've ever seen. It is so big, in fact, that Nick and I had to take a bus clear across town to even get *near* the neighborhood of Seventeenth Street. We took the bus, hardly speaking the whole way, Nick with his face turned to the window like I was a total stranger. So who needed him? All I needed was my mother— well, not my mother, but to find out about my mother. And I was on my way. Although as I sat there—Nick not speaking, me not speaking—I began to wonder: Why was I trying so hard to find out about her? I couldn't get her back. So what was it exactly that I was looking for?

Just information? Or something else? What did I want?

Dummy! I told myself. A fine time to be asking yourself that question now that you've come all the way out here.

I took a deep breath and looked around at the people on the bus and then continued to just sit there, ignoring Nick just the way he was ignoring me. Although by the time we'd been on the bus for almost an hour, I couldn't resist at least one comment.

"Boy!" I said. "I thought my mother went to school in L.A., but I think we're closing in on the Grand Canyon."

Nick didn't answer—not even a shrug.

So I couldn't resist it. "Of course," I added, "you'd probably charge more for a trip to the Grand Canyon."

At that he whirled around to me. "You know," he said, "eavesdropping is a very unattractive habit."

"It wasn't eavesdropping," I said sweetly. "It was overhearing. I know all you care about is your precious minibike. You obviously have no sense of . . . historical perspective."

"Well, I didn't ask for the money!" he said. "Phil just—"

And just at that moment, I saw it out the window —Washington Boulevard! Washington and Seventeenth!

"That's us!" I yelled. I jumped up. "We're here!"

"Getting off, please!" Nick said, pushing his way through the crowd.

"Excuse us," I said. "It's very important."

We jumped down from the bus and stood there looking around as the bus pulled away in a cloud of exhaust.

We were at the corner of Washington and Seventeenth Street. I could see the street sign.

But although I looked at all four corners, nowhere was there a school. Nothing. Nothing but a park.

I turned to Nick, and he shrugged. Were we in the wrong place?

I turned back, looking again in all four directions, but nothing! Just a park. Till I saw something: across the grass was a big marker shaped like the podiums they use in auditoriums.

Together Nick and I walked over to it.

Together we bent and read the little sign under glass: "Wilson High School once stood on this spot. Burned down, September 15, 19–"

Burned down. Gone. My mother's school, all the yearbooks—gone.

"I guess they had no sense of historical perspective, either," Nick muttered.

I could feel my eyes tear over. I couldn't stand this! I had come all this way, and the school was gone.

I plopped down on the grass and dumped out all the stuff from my backpack, looking for . . .

I stopped. Looking for what? I'd been so sure I could find her here, through the yearbook. That was the way to find people from schools, the way to find out about her, what she was like—even Dad had said so!

"Vada," Nick said to me.

I didn't answer, just began rummaging again through my stuff. For what? Why? To do something, to find something . . .

"Vada!" Nick said again. "Now, calm down."

"Right!" I said, looking up at him. "Just calm down. And what am I supposed to do—spend the rest of my time here walking around town looking for someone in a Wilson High School letter sweater or something? I was counting on this school, counting on the yearbook!"

I had to turn away. I couldn't let him see me about to cry.

"Hey!" he said, crouching down beside me. "Calm down. We just have to ask ourselves where yearbooks come from."

"They come from schools!" I said.

"And where else?" he said.

"I don't know what you mean," I said.

"Well," he answered, "they don't just appear out of thin air."

I looked up at him.

He was smiling, a nice smile, sweet—kind, even. "They get printed somewhere, right?" he said.

I jumped up and although I didn't actually hug him, I did give him a big smile. And the next part, as they say, is history.

We found a phone booth with a phone book and went through what seemed like a thousand Yellow Pages and called a hundred printers and finally found one, just one—or at least, just one so far—who said they printed yearbooks.

Was it my lucky day or what? The guy on the phone yelled—he yelled because there was so much noise in the background—that yes, they printed yearbooks, and yes, they kept copies in a warehouse, and yes, we could come and look at them, but no, he wouldn't help us look.

Yes! I couldn't believe it. A warehouse of yearbooks.

We had to take another bus but not nearly as far. I had to admit to myself that I was beginning to be very glad I had Nick along. I'd never have found my way around by myself. Eventually we arrived at this huge old building. The guy at the front desk was small, grimy, mean-looking, and old, but when I explained what I was looking for and why, he led Nick and me into the back of the building into this huge room, where there were stacks and stacks of books on shelves.

"Thanks!" I said to him. "This is really nice of you."

He smiled, and he didn't look so mean anymore. It was kind of a sad smile. "No problem," he said. "I had a mother once myself."

I had a mother once, too. But would I ever find her here? There must have been a million books.

I looked at Nick and he looked at me, and all that good feeling we had had before seemed gone. He looked as surly as ever.

"You're on your own," the old guy said, looking from one to the other of us. "If you find it, you can keep it. We stopped printing yearbooks back in 'sixty-four, so if it's in here at all, it's in the back two rows." He raised a hand at us, a so-long wave. "Happy hunting!" he said.

He left us there, in that dirty, confusing room, with shelves that reached almost to the ceiling —shelves just loaded with books. When Nick and I walked to the back, I saw that the two back shelves must have held a thousand books just by themselves.

Nick and I stared at them. There was a ladder there, and Nick took a few steps up.

I was feeling very depressed, but Nick turned and looked down at me with a smile, suddenly seeming very proud of himself. "Aren't you going to tell me I'm a genius?" he said.

"I wasn't planning to," I answered.

Nick smiled at me again, like he could turn the charm on and off at will. "But it was my calm, thoughtful brilliance that got us here. Go ahead, say it: I'm a genius."

"Tell you what," I said. "I'll say genius if you find Wilson High School, 1954."

For a long time we went through books. The good thing was that there seemed to be some order—in years, that is—so right away we were able to find 1954. The bad thing was that a zillion yearbooks were published in 1954, and this library, or whatever it was, kept them in no alphabetical order at all. That meant you had to pull out each one, read the cover to see what school it was, and stick it back in.

I sneezed about a zillion times and looked at about a zillion books.

But *I found it*. I was the one who found it!

Nick was in the middle of complaining to me about a needle in a haystack and how he had never understood that saying before now, and we were just wasting our time, when I found it! *I found it.*

"It's here!" I yelled. "Omigosh, it's here!"

I grinned up at him. "Genius!" I said. "Genius, genius."

He grinned, too, and hurried down the ladder.

I ran with the book over to a window, with Nick following, and we both plopped down on the floor. I flipped through the book—*J*'s, *K*'s, *L*'s, *M*'s, Martin, McVay—Muldovan!

Muldovan. Maggie Muldovan.

I could not believe I was holding it—holding it. My mother when she wasn't much older than me.

"Look!" I breathed. "It's her."

I studied her picture, her smile, the tilt of her head. She was beautiful—a little different from her passport, but not much, although her hair was much longer here.

My mother in high school.

And then I read: "Margaret Ann Muldovan, Newspaper, Literary Magazine, French Club, Drama Club, Chorus, Girls' Basketball, Swim Team. With Maggie's combo of good looks and talent, we're sure to be seeing her name in lights."

I took a deep breath.

Yes, even then. She was going to be famous. She was going to achieve.

"Yearbooks always set you up for disappointment," Nick said, reading over my shoulder. "I want mine to say, 'Nick probably won't amount to much, so don't be surprised if you never hear anything about him again.'"

I heard him but hardly heard him. I was looking for some sign, some hint of who my mother's best friend would have been, someone she'd hung out with. Maybe someone else in the drama club. Or on the newspaper! Yes. She loved to read and write, just like me.

"This going to take long?" Nick said. "The smell in here is killing me."

I stood up. "It's the leather," I said.

"Smells like gym bags," he said.

"Leather," I said. "I love the smell of leather bindings."

"I love the smell of chili dogs," Nick said.

"I'm ready now," I said, and I tucked the yearbook under my arm.

And we were out of there. Out of there with my mother's yearbook. Out of there with somewhere to go, some connection to find.

For the second time that day I felt like hugging Nick.

_____ CHAPTER

X

_F_ ortunately—unfortunately?—that feeling didn't last too long. We had to go through more phone books and more lists of names before finally we found someone who would remember her, or at least someone we thought _might_ remember her. So now we were on another bus, on our way to Daryl Tanaka's office, Daryl who used to be the editor of the high school newspaper and whose office was halfway across town. Thank goodness Shelly had given me extra money, so I didn't have to rely on Nick to pay for all these buses and stuff.

As we sat on the bus, we continued to look through the yearbook, trying to find the names of other people who were in the same clubs with my mom. Mostly we found girls, except for this Daryl guy and Stanley Rosenfeld, the newspaper photographer, and

Peter Webb in drama. How come more guys didn't take part in clubs?

"The guys will be easier to find," Nick said. "Girls change their names if they get married."

"I'd never do that," I said.

"Get married?" Nick said.

"Change my name," I said.

"You mean you think the guy should change his name?" Nick said in this challenging tone of voice.

"I don't think anybody should change their names," I said. "That way, you can always find them when you need them."

"What if they don't want to be found?" Nick said.

I glared at him. "Why do you argue with everything I say?"

He just shrugged and looked away. We rode in silence to our destination.

But when we got to that business address, we were in for another surprise—although fortunately it wasn't a this-place-has-burned-down surprise, like the last one. The surprise was that this business address was a police station. And the person we were looking for, Daryl Tanaka? Turns out he's a policeman.

The person at the desk didn't even ask what we wanted when I asked if Daryl Tanaka worked there. She just yelled, "Hey, Daryl. You got company," and nodded toward a desk in the center of a big room, where a policeman was sitting.

As we walked across to him, I was nervous—

nervous, but excited, too. I leaned in close to Nick. "This is a miracle!" I said.

"What do you mean, 'miracle'?"

"It's a miracle his aunt was home and knew where he worked and told us where his office is."

"There's only three Tanakas in the phone book," Nick said. "One of them was bound to work out. A miracle is like winning the Irish Sweepstakes when you didn't even buy a ticket."

"But that could never happen," I said.

"But if it did, it would sure be a miracle."

Why did he always argue with me?

By then we were standing in front of Sergeant Daryl Tanaka's desk.

I had already rehearsed most of what I wanted to say to him, and it all came out in a rush as we sat down—sat down across the desk from this stern-faced guy who just stared straight at me the whole time I was talking, not smiling, not nodding, not anything.

I blurted out the whole story about my mother and trying to find out about her, and about my school project, and about coming out here, and about the yearbook and the burned-down school, and I talked too much, till eventually, I just wound down.

"So," I said, "I just thought maybe you could tell me something about her. You do remember her?"

He nodded. "Yes, and it's too bad about your mom, but at least she went peacefully. I've seen a lot of people go out the hard way."

"What do you remember about her?" I asked.

"Well," Daryl said, "we worked on the paper together. I never agreed with a single thing she said or did, but she was really something. In the fifties, you did what they told you. You bought the whole deal. But not Maggie! At graduation, some big deal congressman said that McCarthy was the greatest American ever lived, and know what Maggie did? She gets up in front of five hundred people and walks out. *Out!* A couple of people followed her. It took a lot of guts, I'll tell you."

"Wow!" I said. "And you walked out with my mom?"

He leaned across the desk to me. "You kidding?" he said. "My parents would have shot me. I was president of the Young Republicans. I was Japanese-American, first generation. I was hall monitor. I didn't want to start World War Three."

I just stared at him, but Nick said, "You saved a lot of lives. You should be proud."

Daryl gave Nick a deadly look.

Boy, I thought, I'd hate to mess with him!

But I didn't want him to get off track, either, so I quick reached in my backpack, pulled something out, and handed it to him—the paper bag with the date on it.

"Maybe this will mean something to you?" I said, handing it across the desk to him. "My mother saved it years ago."

Daryl rolled his eyes. "It's a little late for finger-prints," he said.

"I know!" I said. "But I'm trying to find out her

greatest achievement. Maybe it was something that happened on this date. If she did one amazing thing that nobody else did."

For a long minute Daryl was quiet, and I took the opportunity to look around the room.

On the desk, half facing me, was a picture—Daryl with his entire family, all dressed in police uniforms. It was a family of cops!

But there was something else interesting about the picture. On the bottom, in the corner, it said, "Stanley Rosenfeld Photo Studios"—and we already knew that Stanley Rosenfeld was the photographer for the school newspaper.

Could it be the same Stanley Rosenfeld? Was that too much of a coincidence?

Could we look him up? Maybe he'd remember my mother.

"Well," Daryl said eventually, looking up at the ceiling, almost smiling, "she was the first girl ever suspended for smoking. Everyone was really surprised when Maggie Muldovan was turned in. She got kicked out for two weeks."

Nick burst out laughing, but I didn't think it was at all funny.

"Smoking!" I said. "Suspended from school? My mother? I don't believe it! I just can't believe that my mother would do anything like that."

"Nobody else could believe it, either," Daryl said, and he actually smiled then.

So what? It wasn't like smoking was a big sin or

anything. And anybody could make a mistake. But I felt terrible. Ridiculous, but I felt like crying.

I snuck a look at Nick, who was looking back at me.

He turned back to Daryl. "What kind of a sleazoid geek would turn her in?" he asked quietly.

"I'd do it again in a minute!" he said proudly.

I stared at him. "You?" I burst out. *"You* ratted on my mother?"

"What are you?" Nick said. "Hitler's hall monitor?"

"Look!" Daryl said, standing up like he was clearly dismissing us. "The law is the law."

He pointed a finger at Nick. "Maybe you should go join a hippie commune," he went on, his jaw tight, "but let me tell you something—sooner or later, it's going to be *your* turn to take out the garbage."

"That's got nothing to do with it!" Nick said, and he didn't stand up, like he wasn't giving an inch. "What about giving the other guy a break? What about—"

"What about living in the real world, pal?" Daryl shot back. "I know your type, all peace and love and brotherhood until somebody rips off your ten-speed. Then you want to give them the chair."

He started out of the office but stopped and turned to me. "A word to the wise, young lady," he said. "I'd be a tad more careful who I hung out with."

And he was gone.

I stood up, and Nick did, too. I saw him eyeing a

pack of cigarettes on Daryl's desk, and I wanted to throw up.

"Great!" I said to him as we went back down the hall. "This'll be great in my report: my mother got suspended for smoking."

"I think it's cool," Nick said.

"You would," I answered.

We went outside and stood on the sidewalk, waiting for another bus, but this time a bus to take us home. I still had more phone calls to make, but it was late and I was exhausted. Besides, I was getting sick of Nick—nice one minute, a real pain the next.

"You mean," Nick said, "you'd rather have a mother who's a member of the police state? Rules are made to be broken."

He nodded in the direction of an appliance store behind us that had about a thousand TV sets in the window, all replaying the Watergate thing with Nixon.

"Just ask him," Nick said, meaning, I guess, President Nixon. "At least your mom was normal."

The bus came and we got on. When we sat down, Nick again turned and stared out the window.

Well, I thought, I personally don't agree that rules are made to be broken. But I reserve the right to bend them when necessary. And I had an idea that I was going to have to do some pretty serious bending if I was going to get what I'd come out here to get.

"Nick?" I said after a minute.

"Hmm?" he said. He didn't turn away from the

window, but at least he answered me—an improvement over this morning.

"Did you see the picture on the desk?" I asked.

He turned to face me. "Yeah," he said. "Cop family!"

"That's not what I meant," I said. "It said, 'Stanley Rosenfeld Photo Studios,' and since Stanley Rosenfeld was the school newspaper photographer, I thought maybe he still lived in L.A. It seemed to be a recent picture of Daryl."

Nick shrugged. "It would be a long shot," he said.

"But not a miracle?" I said, almost smiling.

He actually smiled back. "No," he said, "a miracle would be—"

I held up one hand. "I know!" I said. "I know already!"

CHAPTER

XI

*T*he next day two things happened, one good, one not so good. The good was that the Stanley Rosenfeld Photo Studios *was* run by the same Stanley Rosenfeld who was in high school with my mother. He was doing a wedding the following afternoon, and he said we could come talk to him, as long as we didn't interfere with his picture-taking. And when I told him who I was and why I wanted to see him, he kept saying, "Maggie! I can't believe it! Maggie."

I explained to him at least three times that I wasn't Maggie, just Maggie's daughter, and I know he must have understood, but still he kept murmuring, "Maggie."

I was very excited to be going to meet him.

The bad was what happened just before we left. Well, maybe it wasn't bad, but I could see it made Uncle Phil upset. And I hate to see Uncle Phil upset.

We were just getting ready to leave and had come down to the garage to say good-bye—both Nick and me, because for some reason Nick wanted to go see this Stanley guy, too—when a man drove in with this really flashy car, a car Nick couldn't stop staring at. Uncle Phil and Gomez, who works with him, even they looked up for a moment from their work to stare at it. It was this shiny red Jaguar XK150—and does that sound like I'm getting to know about cars or not? If I stayed here long enough, I'd know as much as Uncle Phil.

Anyway, this guy drove in, this really cool-looking guy with a deep tan and a smile—and I mean a *smile.* One of those practiced TV smiles, like Judy had used on Kevin Phillips that day.

As soon as the guy saw Rose, he got out of the car and went over to her.

"Well, hello!" he said, and he held out his hand. "I'm Sam Helburn." His voice was a lot like his smile—practiced.

There was just a second's pause before Rose took his hand. Then she shook hands briefly and let his drop.

"I'm staying at the Chateau," he went on, still smiling. "The guy who runs the garage said you're the best Jag people in town."

Rose smiled back at him as though he had finally said the right thing. "Well, Enrique's great, and we are the best."

"Then I've come to the right place," he said.

Nick began walking slowly around the car, running his hand over it gently, like it was a wild animal he was trying to tame.

"I guess you have," Rose said. She flipped open her clipboard to the work order and started writing. "So," she said, "what's wrong?"

"Nothing," Sam said. "Nothing at all."

Rose didn't even roll her eyes. "I mean with your car," she said sweetly.

"Oh," Sam said. "Just an oil change. I just drove in from Chicago and . . . nice hair."

"Excuse me?" Rose said.

"I was commenting on your hair," Sam answered.

I turned and looked toward Uncle Phil, but he wasn't looking back. He was bent over, buried under a car hood. Good thing, too.

With my head I tried to signal Nick to come with me, but he didn't notice. Clearly he had fallen in love. With the car. I didn't even exist.

"Oh?" Rose said. "Are you a hairdresser?"

"Pediatric cardiologist," he answered.

"You mean you fix the hearts of little babies?"

Sam nodded. "Mostly little babies. But not exclusively."

Wow! I thought. What a neat thing to do. Although I knew if it were me, I'd love the babies. And faint at the first sight of blood.

I guess Rose thought it was neat, too, because she closed the clipboard and leaned against the car like she was ready to talk awhile.

I walked around the car to Nick. "Come on," I said. "Let's go."

"In a minute," he said. "Have you ever seen such a car?"

He kept on stroking it, petting it. I mean, he *had* fallen in love.

What is it with guys and cars?

Behind us, Sam and Rose were going on, something about Sam teaching and it being a good relief from the operating room, blah, blah, blah, when Uncle Phil strolled up and leaned against the car, right beside Rose, real casual like.

Nick stopped petting the car and grinned at me. "This should be interesting," he said softly.

"Hi, I'm Phil Sultenfuss," Phil said. "Is there some kind of problem?"

Rose turned to him. "No problem," she said. "Dr. Helburn needs his oil changed, that's all."

Phil nodded. "I see," he said. "Usually that doesn't require such a lengthy consultation."

"Rose is being very thorough," Sam said.

"Rose?" Phil said.

Just that one word, but you could tell what he meant.

Rose knew, too. She opened her clipboard again. "Why don't you come in tomorrow, Dr. Helburn?" she said. "We open at eight, if that's not too early."

"I'll be here," he said.

He made a gesture, sort of like a little salute, his hand just brushing Rose's arm as he let it drop. Then he gave her that smile again and climbed into that incredible car. Nick and I moved away as he pulled out.

"What's with the touching?" Phil said the minute Sam Helburn was gone. "Why was he touching you?"

"He wasn't touching me; he was gesturing," Rose answered.

"He was caressing!" Phil said.

"Oh, Philip!" Rose said. "For heaven's sake."

"I don't think you want to involve heaven in this," Phil said, "because I think God saw even more than I did."

"Philip!" Rose said. "If you want the rights of a husband, there's something you got to ask me. If not, you're going to have to get accustomed to the rights of what you are."

"Oh?" Phil said, and I recognized that deadly sound in his voice that he gets when he's mad. "And what is that?"

"A close friend with mechanical skills," she answered.

Uncle Phil turned away from her, heading back to his work with Gomez, but it was clear he was still addressing her as he went. "Anyone with taste," he said from between gritted teeth, "anyone with breeding—a *gentleman*—would choose British racing green. With maybe a tan interior."

"Philip, please!" Rose yelled.

"But," Phil went on, as if Rose hadn't even spoken, his voice rising, "when you buy a red car with black interior you've got one thing on your mind and one thing only. And I'm too much of a gentleman to say what that one thing is in front of the children."

Which I guess meant us.

Well, we were going, anyway.

Yes, because Rose was glaring at Nick, who just shrugged. "Hey, don't mind us," he said.

Together we left for the address Stanley had given me on the phone.

Once outside, Nick was quiet, as though he was thinking.

"What?" I said.

He just shrugged. "Oh, nothing. But I kind of like Phil."

I smiled. I do too.

"It was just a little tiff," I said. "They'll get over it."

He nodded. "Maybe."

We walked about a zillion miles, not talking much, but not mad either, the way we were yesterday, just quiet. Nick said no buses went in the direction of the wedding place, so we had no choice but to walk. "When I have enough money for my minibike," he said, and he didn't even blush, "then I can ride it to places like this."

I wondered if Uncle Phil was paying him for today, too.

We finally got there, to this very fancy-looking place, like a hotel or country club or something. It made me a little nervous, because I've never been in such a fancy place.

Inside, it was clear from the music that a wedding reception was taking place in the back, and we followed the sound.

There, in this huge crowded room, a big party was going on, with a bride and groom and people all dressed up in fancy clothes, dancing and having their pictures taken. The photographer was this funny-looking squat little man who followed each couple around, making friendly comments to them.

Stanley Rosenfeld. The man who used to know my mother!

"Okay, Esther, you gorgeous thing, you, smile for the birdie!" he called to one couple as we walked up behind him. "Hold it! Hold it! Beauteeful!"

They blinked in the glare of the camera flash as I said, "Mr. Rosenfeld? Stanley?"

He turned to me.

"Oh!" he said. With both hands he clasped the camera to his chest as if he was holding on to his heart. "You've got to be her daughter!"

I nodded. "Vada," I said. "I'm Vada. Maggie's daughter."

"Those eyes!" he said. "I would have known you anywhere. Who would believe—Maggie's daughter. Maggie!"

"Were you good friends?" I asked.

He smiled. "Yeah, from the time we were little. Your mother was something special, I can tell you. Really something special." He leaned in close, like he was telling me a secret. "You're going to be just like her. To tell the truth, I had quite a crush on her."

"You did?" I said.

He nodded. "Who didn't? She could do everything!"

"Everything?" I said. "Like what?"

I looked at Nick, hoping he was getting all this.

"Everything!" He waved a hand. "She played basketball, she danced like an angel, she . . ." He sighed and shook his head. "And then she'd look at you with those big blue eyes and you'd be gone, swept into her spell. I asked her out a couple of times, but she always said no."

He turned away, then stopped another dancing couple.

Did he feel bad when she said no? He must have. But she probably did like him—just not as a boyfriend but as a friend.

The way I was with Thomas J.

Stanley snapped some more pictures, then turned back to us. "But I was her friend," he said. "When her parents passed away, we were both in grade school. Well, I guess you know all this."

I shook my head. "No!" I said. "She died when I was born. So I hardly know anything. That's why I'm out here. I want to find out every single thing I can, from everybody who ever knew her. But I only have five days—no, four more days to do it in."

"Well, I didn't know her as well when we got older," he said. "Like I said, she'd never go out with me. But her grandmother raised her and—"

"Grandmother?" I said. "Where? Do you know where she lived?"

Stanley nodded. "Sure. The Longwood Apartments. Over on Laurel, right near Fountain."

"I know where that is," Nick said.

"Yeah," Stanley went on, "I remember those days well. Then we all went to college, UCLA, and Maggie started hanging out with the drama department types. There was this one guy, Peter Webb, he's a big director now. He knew her well."

"Peter Webb," I said, repeating it, memorizing it. "Do you know his number?"

"Nah," Stanley said. "Peter's out of my league. He's got a big deal at one of the studios. The only reason I even knew him is we all took this poetry class together with this crazy guy. Alfred Boderfelder."

"Beidermeyer!" I said. "You mean, Alfred Beidermeyer?"

"That's it, Beidermeyer. What a nut!"

"You knew him?" I said. "You actually *knew* him?"

"Everybody did," Stanley said. "Walk along Citrus between Fountain and Sunset on any afternoon. If he's still alive, he'll be there, sitting under a small palm tree—well, maybe by now it's a big palm tree—right in front of his house."

"I know Citrus and Fountain," Nick said. "That should be easy to find. It's only a few blocks from here."

"He'll remember my mother for sure," I said, looking at Nick. "She loved poetry and writing. I'll bet she stood out in that class."

"Well," Stanley said, "it was a pretty big class —Foundations of Poetic Thought, I think it was called, and he was pretty old even then." He took a deep breath. "But then, who could forget our Maggie?"

The band changed from a slow dance to a fast one, and Stanley said, "I should get back to work."

"Just one more thing," I said. I dug in my backpack and took out the little paper bag. Again. "Does this mean anything to you?" I asked, handing it to him.

He turned it over in his hands. "No," he said, a kind of wistful look on his face. "But I wish it did."

I took the bag back. "Thanks for all your help, Mr. Rosenfeld," I said. "And . . . and I'm sorry my mother wouldn't go out with you."

I smiled at him and he smiled back. "I'm sure she would have had a wonderful time," I said.

"Just like Maggie," he said softly, and then he turned back to the dancers, calling to them to turn and smile at the birdie.

Nick and I made our way out of there. I was glad to get away from the noise and the crowded room, glad to have some time to think.

I had met one more person who had known my mother. One more person who liked her.

Well, I guess Daryl didn't like her. But he admired her.

I was collecting more little bits. More and more, until finally I would know something big, something important. I would put all the bits together. Until finally I would know my mother.

CHAPTER

XII

*W*e were on Citrus, walking slowly, looking up and down the street for a little or big palm tree with someone sitting under it. The street was narrow and steep, with the houses perched atop it and long, long steps to climb to the houses from the street.

I was so excited, I couldn't stand it. To actually *meet* Alfred Beidermeyer. Meet him and know he knew my mother!

"This is the street he walks down every day," I said to Nick, thinking that maybe my mother had walked here, too. "And for inspiration—"

"Boy, you're really into this, aren't you," Nick said.

He sounded bored again, but who cared? If I could actually meet Alfred Beidermeyer . . .

"It's him!" I said, spotting an old, old man sitting under a palm tree—a small palm tree. Behind him was an archway, and through it you could see another steep flight of steps up to a Spanish-looking adobe building.

"Bet it's not," Nick said.

"Bet it is!" I said. "Look. He's writing!"

We both stopped and looked. It *had* to be him. A tiny, frail old man sitting on a metal folding chair with a briefcase balanced on a small folding table. The briefcase was open, and inside it was a kitchen timer. The man was wearing worn pants and a heavy tweed jacket, even though the day was awfully warm. But it had to be him. Because he was writing.

I couldn't help staring. I just knew Alfred Beidermeyer was writing a beautiful poem, and I bet the timer had something to do with it. Maybe it was his way of being sure he kept to a writing schedule.

"Well," Nick said, "are you just going to stand and stare?"

Yes. Because I didn't know what else to do. What could I possibly say to Alfred Beidermeyer, who actually knew my mother?

But I had to say something, had to start the conversation somehow. Slowly I approached him. And came out with something totally brilliant. "Hello," I said.

He didn't even look up. "If you're selling Girl Scout cookies," he said, "I'm a borderline diabetic."

"You're Alfred Beidermeyer, aren't you?" I said.

At that he looked up. "You had to remind me?"

"I'm Vada Sultenfuss," I said. "And this is my

friend Nick Zigmund." I nodded toward his pad of paper. "Are you writing a poem?"

"No," he said. "I'm writing the phone company because they keep charging me for calls to Caracas, Venezuela." He looked from me to Nick. "Do you know anybody in Caracas, Venezuela?" he asked.

"No," I said, shaking my head.

"No," Nick said.

"Neither do I," Mr. Beidermeyer said.

The bell rang suddenly—the little timer in his briefcase—and he picked it up and turned it off. "'Ask not for whom the bell tolls,'" he murmured, and began collecting his papers. "Time for my pills and my nap."

He started to get up, but as he did, his briefcase slid sideways and papers scattered all over.

Nick bent to gather them as Mr. Beidermeyer grabbed for the folding chair. He must have bumped the table as he did, because it suddenly collapsed.

"I can handle it," Mr. Beidermeyer said to Nick, but as he lifted the chair, it fell open.

"We'll help bring everything in, if you want," Nick said.

"So, help!" Mr. Beidermeyer said, letting me take the chair.

And did he need help! With his head he gestured through the archway to the house behind, where there was a steep flight of steps leading up to what must have been his apartment. And I mean *steep*. Did he go up and down those stairs every day?

Nick and I climbed up, carrying the briefcase and

95

the papers and the chair and table, and very slowly he followed us. *Very* slowly. We got to the top first, and waited. From below us, we could actually *hear* him gasping.

"If he has a heart attack and dies," Nick said quietly, "you're carrying the body down yourself."

I didn't even bother to answer him. This was Alfred Beidermeyer he was joking about! Alfred Beidermeyer, who really shouldn't be climbing these stairs. I watched him come up, my heart pounding in my throat. I even had this ridiculous picture in my head of me going down and carrying him up, but of course I didn't.

When Mr. Beidermeyer finally reached the top of the stairs, gasping and hanging on to the railing, I tried to say something cheerful. "At least you get plenty of exercise," I said brightly.

"It keeps me young," he gasped. But he looked near death.

Inside, he collapsed into a chair by the door, rubbing one knee.

I took a look around. The apartment was tiny, with one tiny room that opened into another tiny room, both of them cluttered—books and papers everywhere. It was like being in a library—no, like being in a poet's home. A great poet's home. I breathed in deeply and smiled. This was exactly what my place would look like someday.

Next to me, Nick muttered, "What a mess!"

I gave him a dirty look and turned back to Mr.

Beidermeyer. "Do you still teach?" I asked, trying to sound casual but feeling my heart pounding hard. Because now was the time to find out what I had come here to find.

"Gave it up years ago," he answered, still rubbing his knee. "Actually, it gave me up."

"My mother was in your class once," I said. "Foundations of Poetic Thought, at UCLA?"

He sighed. "UCLA. My cardigan sweater period."

"Maybe you'll remember her?" I said, practically holding my breath. "Her name . . ." I swallowed. "Her name was Maggie Muldovan."

Mr. Beidermeyer didn't answer.

Forever. I waited forever. And when he still didn't answer, I tried again. "Do you remember her?" I asked.

"I've been blessed with a bad memory," he answered.

Blessed?

"But see," I said, moving closer to him so he could look up and see for himself. "People say she looked just like me."

He didn't look at me. He did stand up, though, and limp over to his desk, where there was a row of pill bottles. Very methodically he took one pill from each bottle, then downed them all with a glass of water that was right there. "I wasn't too well in those days," he said, his back to us. "I'm not too well now."

Meaning if he wasn't well, he couldn't remember?

Then I thought of something—a way to make him remember. Surely my mother loved his poetry and his class and let him know that? "My mother?" I said. "I'm sure my mother found your lectures fascinating."

"I doubt it," he said cheerfully. "Writers are notoriously boring."

"No, they're not!" I said. "I want to be a writer. I want to be just like you!"

"Me!" Mr. Beidermeyer turned and looked at me then, but there was no recognition in his face. "My dear, this is not a country that rewards poetry. This is a country that rewards gas mileage. Besides, people don't read poems anymore. They watch TV. Don't be a writer, be a TV repairman."

Don't be a writer! *He* was a writer. He was a wonderful writer!

"Mr. Beidermeyer," I said. "I don't think you realize how much people care about you."

Mr. Beidermeyer rubbed his forehead with his thumb, and when he answered, I wasn't sure what his answer had to do with what I had just said.

"I've got a son in Greenwich, Connecticut," he said, a puzzled look on his face. "He tells me he has a nice apartment for me over his garage. Given the choice of carbon monoxide and forty-two steps, I took the steps."

"But the steps keep you young," Nick said softly, speaking to Mr. Beidermeyer for the first time since we came up. I thought he sounded sad.

Mr. Beidermeyer waved his hand. "Ah!" he said. "I stopped wanting to be young. I stopped fighting it. That's why I stopped writing."

"You stopped writing!" I said, staring at him. "You can't stop writing. You have to write. Dylan Thomas said it, said you have to rage against the dying of the light. You can't stop writing!"

"Dylan Thomas?" Mr. Beidermeyer said. "Now, that name rings a bell."

He began rummaging through the mess on his desk and after a moment fished something out and handed it to me—a small, worn-looking paper.

I took it from him. A note, a handwritten note. I read: "'I was moved and inspired. With best wishes, Dylan Thomas.'"

I was holding a handwritten note—from Dylan Thomas! Really!

I looked from the note to Mr. Beidermeyer.

He shrugged. "It was for the cover of my new collection, except they're not publishing it. My editor got a job with 'The Bionic Woman.'"

I couldn't believe it. Not publishing it! Not publishing Alfred Beidermeyer? That was a terrible, awful thing to do to him.

Even if he didn't remember my mother.

I felt tears come to my eyes, but Mr. Beidermeyer didn't seem upset at all.

He went over to his couch and began fluffing up a pillow, obviously ready for his nap.

"I think we should go," Nick said softly.

"Mr. Beidermeyer," I said. "Are you . . ,"

But I didn't finish my question because I didn't know what it was I wanted to ask. Are you sad? Upset? Of course he was sad.

Or was he? He didn't look it.

I was, though. But why? And how could they *not* publish his poetry? How could he give up writing? He would die! Even Dylan Thomas had said he shouldn't give up.

He had given up writing.

And he didn't remember my mother.

Mr. Beidermeyer began settling himself on his bed, a dreamy kind of smile on his face.

Yes. We should go.

"Thank you for your time, Mr. Beidermeyer," I said. "I'm sorry if we disturbed you."

"Didn't disturb me," he said. "I appreciate the help with the chair."

"No problem," Nick answered.

"And good luck with the phone company," I said as I turned to the door.

Behind me I thought I heard Mr. Beidermeyer laugh, but I didn't mean it as a joke or anything.

We left, going down that crazy flight of stairs, Nick holding my arm like I was blind or as old as Mr. Beidermeyer or something.

Did he know I was fighting back tears?

Did he know that I had absolutely no idea why I wanted to cry?

Downstairs on the street, I didn't speak, and

neither did Nick. But after a moment, Nick said, "Come on."

He took my hand and started to pull me along. "Let's go," he said. "I know what to do. I'll take you to the place I always go when I need cheering up."

CHAPTER

XIII

*H*ere we are!" Nick said, after we had walked a few blocks.

We turned from the street onto a pathway where there was a sign: La Brea Tar Pits! Prehistoric Creatures Perished Here.

We walked all along this high walkway till we were looking down on a huge pit of black tar surrounded by a tall, tall fence.

Down inside the pit were enormous statues of prehistoric creatures that seemed to be stuck in the tar. From the pose of one of them, it seemed to still be struggling to get out.

How awful! The poor creature!

"This is the place!" Nick said. "What do you think?"

I looked from the creatures up to Nick. "You said

you'd take me where you go to be cheered up," I said.

"Yup!" Nick said. "This is the place."

"You get cheered up *here?*" I asked.

"Sure," Nick said. "Look at it this way. However bad I feel, it isn't as bad as becoming extinct in a bottomless pit of tar."

I shook my head. "And I thought *I* was weird," I muttered.

There was a moment's silence, and then he said, "You *are* weird. I was just trying to cheer you up, but . . . Oh, never mind!" He turned away. "Let's go."

"No!" I said. "Don't. I like that you brought me here."

He turned back, but clearly he was mad, or hurt. "Hey, what do I care? Coming from a chick from Pennsylvania who wears a *mood* ring!"

It was very sarcastic the way he said "mood ring."

It was no ordinary mood ring! It was my memory of Thomas J.

"This isn't *just* a mood ring!" I answered.

"Does it work?" Nick said.

Work! I made a face at him. "Well," I said, "it doesn't open cans or anything, but . . ."

I looked down at it and sighed, twisting it around my finger. How could I explain how special it was? Or what the memories were?

"I don't know if it works or not," I said. "I wear it because it's a reminder of a friend of mine."

Nick stuck his hands in his jeans pockets and looked down into the tar pits. "A boyfriend?" he said real casually.

"Well," I said, "he was a boy and he was a friend. He was my best friend. When we were kids, we were going to move out here and live with the Brady Bunch. Then I lost this ring in the woods. And when he went to find it, he was stung by bees and died."

"Wow!" Nick said. "I'm sorry."

I nodded. I was sorry too. Weird, how much I still missed Thomas J.

Nick kept staring into the pit. "Do you feel like your friend's up in heaven now, looking down, watching you all the time?"

I didn't think it was meant to be funny, the way he said it, more like he was asking a real question.

I nodded. "I do think that sometimes," I said. I couldn't help smiling. "But," I added, "I hope he's not watching me *all* the time."

Nick turned to me. "Can I try it?" he said, holding out his hand for the ring. "See if it changes colors on me."

Should I? I hardly ever took it off my hand. But he'd be careful, I was sure.

"Okay," I said, "but be careful. It has a lot of value to me."

Carefully I slipped the ring off my finger and handed it to him, holding my hand underneath it to catch it in case he dropped it.

He didn't drop it, though. But when he tried to put it on, he couldn't even get it over his first knuckle.

"Maybe it'll fit my pinky," he said.

"Don't force it!" I said. "You'll break it."

"I won't break it," he said, turning slightly away from me so I couldn't see what he was doing. "I just want to see it turn colors."

But what if he did break it? It's all I have of Thomas J. And if it was broken . . .

I couldn't stand this. "I want it back!" I said, reaching around him for it. "I never should have taken it off."

"Relax!" he said, turning back to me. "Oh, no!" he yelled, and he looked down.

"Oh, no, what?" I said.

"I think I dropped it."

"You *think?*" I said.

I pulled his hand toward mine and looked inside —it was empty.

I looked up at him, and he was looking down at the tar pits, the bubbling tar pits.

"In there?" I said, my heart beginning to thump so hard in my throat I could barely speak.

"Look," he said. "It was an accident. I'll get you a new one. I'll—"

But I took off running, down the steps, down toward the pits. It might still be on the path. It *couldn't* have rolled in. Please.

I reached the bottom of the steps and turned to see Nick racing down after me.

I looked everywhere, up and down the path. But no ring. Oh, God, don't let it have fallen in, please don't let it have fallen in, I prayed. I climbed up on the fence to look, feeling tears streaming down my face.

Nick came up from behind and grabbed me around the waist. "You can't do that!" he yelled.

"Leave me alone!" I yelled back. "It's all I have of Thomas J. I have to get my ring!"

I struggled to get away, but Nick held tight. "You mean this ring?" he said.

He held it out to me—my ring. My mood ring. Thomas J's ring.

I stepped back from the fence. Then, very calmly, I took the ring back and put it on. And then, before he even knew what was coming, I began pounding at him, actually pummeling him with my fists, while he tried to hold me off. "You jerk!" I yelled. "You idiot!"

I was crying. Really crying. He *was* a jerk. A mean one. I would never trust him again.

But then something weird began happening. For some reason, as we continued half fighting, half wrestling with each other, I began laughing just a little—laughing and crying all at the same time.

But then, after a while, mostly laughing. Because he was holding me, and I was pounding on him, and then, after a while, I wasn't pounding him anymore —yet he was still holding me.

So why was I laughing? And why was he still holding me?

He looked at me and I looked at him. And then I pulled away and we were both quiet for a while.

"That was mean," I said finally.

"I meant it as a joke," he answered, but I was happy to see that he looked embarrassed. "You hit pretty hard."

"I know I do, but it was still mean," I said.

"Can I make it up to you?" he asked.

"No," I said. But then I added, "How?"

"That Peter Webb, the one that Stanley mentioned? Everybody knows him—I mean, doesn't like *know* him but knows who he is. I know where his studio is. And they give tours. Tomorrow I'll take you on the studio tour. Maybe that way we can get in to see him."

"Now!" I said. "Let's do it now."

Nick shook his head. "Too late. The tours are over for the day. Tomorrow? Will you forgive me if I take you tomorrow?"

"If you take me tomorrow," I said. "Let's go home."

Actually I was glad to be going home. I was exhausted, what with meeting Mr. Beidermeyer and almost losing my special ring and all. So when we got there and reported in to Rose and Phil and had dinner, I was so tired I went to bed practically right away. I wasn't too tired to notice, however, that Rose and Phil were still being cool to each other. And Rose, who always had classical music playing in the background, had turned it up especially loud— maybe to cover the silence.

Later I was lying on my couch and was almost sound asleep when I heard someone tiptoeing through the living room. I opened my eyes sleepily, and through my eyelashes saw Nick heading for the kitchen.

I scrunched my eyes up so they'd look closed, but I watched him from between my lashes. When he got to my couch, he paused for a minute, and I saw him looking down at me.

Was he admiring me? Or was he thinking I was a little pain he had to drag around, be bribed to drag around?

But after that weird thing that happened by the tar pits, when I was pounding on him and he was holding me and we were both laughing, I had a feeling something had changed, that maybe he didn't think I was such a pain.

I sighed and turned over a little, pretending to be asleep. But I tried to be graceful as I turned, and maybe—sexy?

But how can you look sexy in a plain old V-neck shirt with a blanket around your shoulders?

Anyway, I was just thinking that when I heard Rose.

She was whispering, but Rose can't ever really have a quiet voice, so I heard each word she said.

"Nicholas!" she said. "What are you doing up?"

He whispered back. "I'm thirsty."

"There's water in the bathroom," Rose said.

"I want juice," he said.

"Well, don't wake Vada!" she whispered.

"I won't!" he said back as he went into the kitchen and opened the refrigerator.

I smiled. I bet anything I knew why he wanted juice, not water.

I bet anything he had come through the living room to look at me.

And then I thought: I am weird. I am definitely weird.

Just last week I had told myself that I'd never have anything to do with boys, never be like Judy and Kevin. And here I was liking that Nick was looking at me.

I wondered if my mother ever felt like this.

CHAPTER
XIV

*T*he next day Nick and I left early so we'd be on the first bus tour of the studio. Before we left I tried to see if Phil and Rose had made up, but each was in a separate area of the garage, so there was no way to tell.

Nick and I made it to the studio, and even before noon we were on one of those open-air buses that take you around and show you the sets and the actors. The guy giving the tour was trying to be impressive, but instead he was just kind of gross.

"Look at this!" he called out as the bus rolled through what looked like a snow-covered street in New York City. "Hard to believe there's snow on the ground when it's eighty degrees out, huh? That's the magic of movies, my friends."

I looked at Nick, and he looked at me, and both of us made throw-up faces.

"He reminds me of my math teacher," Nick whispered.

I turned back to the tour guide. "Excuse me!" I called out. "Can you tell us what stage Peter Webb is filming on?"

"Stage twenty-nine," he answered, pointing down a side street. "Right over there. But it's a closed set. Nobody's allowed in to watch."

Nick and I exchanged looks, and Nick grabbed my hand. "As soon as this bus slows down, we're out of here."

"Right," I said.

"If anyone asks," he said, grinning, "I'm getting carsick."

We inched our way closer to the open rear door.

As soon as the bus slowed down to turn a corner, we jumped out—and took off running.

Behind us I could hear the tour guide yelling, but we didn't stop. We raced to the end of the street and then down a side street and another, turning a few fast corners. We slowed down once we were sure we had lost the tour bus for good. Then we turned around to make our way back to the street and the set the guide had pointed out—the set where Peter Webb would be.

Peter Webb, who would remember and love my mother, just as Stanley Rosenfeld had.

Or would he be like Mr. Beidermeyer? Blessed with a bad memory?

We wove our way through crowds of actors, some

of them wearing long gowns and elaborate powdered wigs, others in tattered rags.

Just a few steps ahead of us a man was striding along, carrying a huge Roman head. He looked like he had just been beheaded.

It took just a few turns to make our way to Stage 29. It was a clearly marked set so huge that it must have covered half a mile. It was also clear they were in the middle of filming. There was this huge sign that said Jewel in the Sand, and people rushing everywhere with cameras and these enormous lights, and some guy yelling and pointing.

But how could we possibly meet Peter Webb? We surely couldn't interrupt the filming. We'd just have to wait. But if it was a closed set, what if someone saw us and threw us out? And how would we know which one was him?

I looked at Nick, and he looked at me, and we both shrugged. I was beginning to get an idea, though.

I took Nick's hand and pulled him back a few steps. "Who's the most important-looking person over there?" I said softly.

"They all look important," Nick said. "Or like they think they are."

"But *most* important?" I said, carefully looking over the people on the set. "The director would be most important, right?"

"Maybe. Maybe not," Nick answered.

"Why do you argue with everything I say?" I answered, repeating our old argument. "Now look there," I said, pointing to a group of people all clustered around one guy in a chair—a director's chair. "That has to be him," I said.

"Maybe. Maybe not," Nick said, but he was grinning at me.

And then somebody yelled, "Cut! Cut!" And somebody else yelled, "Mr. Webb!" And the guy in the chair stood up.

Peter Webb. It had to be Peter Webb.

"It's him," I said to Nick. "Let's go." We both started across the set. "Mr. Webb?" I called. "Mr. Webb?"

He turned to us, glaring, and two of the guys who'd been hanging around him rushed toward us like they were going to hustle us right off the lot.

But I knew it was Peter Webb. I knew he might not remember. I also knew he might not want to remember. But he was my last chance.

"I'm Maggie Muldovan's daughter!" I yelled in his direction.

His face was an angry red. "I don't care who you are!" he yelled back. "I don't care if you're—"

Then he stopped. *"What?"* he said.

I yelled back. "Maggie!" I yelled. "I'm Maggie Muldovan's daughter."

"Whoa!" Peter yelled. "Hold it!"

Everybody seemed to hold it at that moment. The men who had been rushing toward us stopped, and Peter Webb came over to us.

Peter Webb, who definitely remembered my mother.

He stood there looking down at me, still seeming

very mad. "Maggie Muldovan?" he said. "What do you mean, Maggie Muldovan?"

"I'm her daughter?" I said. I was so nervous it came out like a question.

He didn't answer for a moment, just stood there looking at me. "Look at you!" he said finally. "You're Maggie all over again. Come on. Walk with me." He included Nick in his glance.

We all began walking off the set and along a street that seemed very old-fashioned, some foreign street, I figured.

"So what are you doing here?" Peter asked.

As fast as I could, before he could walk us right out of the studio, if that was his plan, I told him the whole story—well, not the whole story because that would have taken days, but about how my mother died when I was born and about the school project and what I was looking for—although to be honest, the longer I stayed in L.A., the less I really knew about what it was I was looking for. But I didn't say that. There was one thing I was sure I wanted to know about, though—my mother's great achievement. So that's what I ended with.

"I'm looking to find out her greatest achievement," I said.

Peter laughed softly. "Greatest achievement, huh?" he said. "That's the kind of question they ask when you haven't done a picture in five years. I think she could have been a major player, though. God knows that face was made for close-ups. Everything was magic with Maggie."

He turned to me and put a hand on my shoulder. "I'm sorry you never got to know her. She was wonderful. I remember one night we were walking down Hollywood Boulevard, and we put our feet in the stars' footprints. You know, like the tourists do. Maggie had the same size feet as Judy Garland. Of course, mine were a perfect match with Orson Welles."

"Of course," Nick said, but I couldn't tell if that was a sarcastic answer or an admiring one.

Somebody ran up to Peter then and interrupted him with something about getting him a gun—I hoped the guy meant for the movie!—and then Peter turned back to me, his hand still resting on my shoulder.

Nick trailed along on Peter's other side, taking in this whole scene, and I could see how impressed he was, not just with Peter, but with everything.

And Nick always tried to look so cool. Ha!

Anyway, after Peter was stopped again—this time about a dress Peter wanted, and again, I hoped it was for the movie—he went on. "Maggie was something. I remember exactly where I was when I heard she'd died. I was directing a 'Playhouse Ninety.' You probably can't imagine me directing TV, can you?"

"Oh, no, sir," I said, wondering what that had to do with my mother. But I did know about remembering where you were and what you were doing when you heard bad news. I remember exactly what I was doing when Dad told me about Thomas J.

I also thought that if Peter remembered, that meant he had loved her, too.

I wanted to ask him that, but for some reason I couldn't. And why did I care if he loved her? Why did I want everybody to have loved her, even Alfred Beidermeyer?

Peter was quiet for a moment and then went on. "Well, we all pay our dues. Anyways, we were going over the shots for the following day, and Hillary called. You should call Hillary Mitchell. She and Maggie were very tight. She's got this funky clothing store over on Melrose. I'd call her for you, but, well, we kind of had this thing going, and it got a little messy."

I sighed. I knew just what he meant. Just like with Phil and Rose.

"I understand," I said.

A tall, thin woman stopped to speak to Peter, and I realized we were taking up a lot of his time. He was very busy, you could see.

But I had one more thing to ask. When the woman left, I reached in my backpack and took out the paper bag with the date. Again. I held it out to him. "Would you know what this is?" I asked.

He took the bag, examined it. "Not really. An audition. An opening. A birthday. It's not my birthday. Who puts dates on paper bags?"

I took the bag back from him. "My mom," I said. "Thanks for your time, Mr. Webb. I know how busy you are. And . . ."

"I was glad to help," he said. "And don't forget

this fall's movie *Jewel in the Sand*. It's going to be huge." He put both hands on my shoulders and then turned me around so I was facing him. "You're Maggie all over again. If you ever want to be a movie star, call me. You've got the face for close-ups, too."

Too. Just like my mother.

I smiled, and Nick and I left.

But I turned and looked back a few times, watching Peter Webb walk away.

Peter Webb had loved my mother, too.

CHAPTER

XV

*W*hen we got home that day, it was clear that Rose and Uncle Phil had made up, a little bit, anyway. They were talking to each other and even laughing some. And they had planned to go to a meeting together that night.

Nick and I had made a plan for that night, too, that night and the next day. The next day we were going to Hillary Mitchell's shop. And that night, well, we had talked about it all the way home on the bus. But it wasn't a plan that we wanted anyone to know about, so we were going to do it when Rose was asleep. But now that they were going out—this was even better!

I felt terribly guilty about it, but Nick kept saying it was no big deal and not to worry. And I did so much want to do it—and see it. I wanted to see the place where my mother had put her feet in Judy

Garland's footsteps. My mother, whose feet were exactly the same size. Nighttime was the only time to see it, Nick had said, what with the lights and the crowds.

But I was still pretty nervous. I mean, at home I had snuck out of the house a couple times by myself when I was little, but this was different.

"Now, don't expect us before eleven," Uncle Phil said, as they were getting ready to leave. "It may even be midnight if we go out for coffee after the meeting."

"There's lots of fruit here for you," Rose said.

"And you know where the fire extinquisher is," Uncle Phil added.

Nick nodded. "If the fruit bursts into flames, I'll be prepared," he said.

Rose laughed, but I was too nervous to laugh, knowing what we planned to do the minute they were gone.

Rose came over and kissed Nick's cheek. "He is just so clever!" she said.

She bent and kissed my cheek then. "You okay, honey?" she said, very softly. "You seem quiet."

I sighed. "I'm just . . ."

A nervous wreck.

"She's just tired," Nick said. "All this sight-seeing."

"Well," Rose said, "get to sleep early and don't open the door for anyone and . . ."

Nick put his hand on his mom's back and practically pushed her to the door.

"Bye!" he said.

"Bye!" Phil said.

"Bye!" we said.

And they were gone.

Gone!

Nick and I went to the window and watched them, walk to the curb and get into Rose's car.

After the car pulled away, Nick turned away from the window and grinned at me. "Liftoff!" he said.

We were out of there. In no time at all we were on the street and around the corner, heading for our destination.

It wasn't much of a walk, fifteen minutes, maybe, and we were there—there in front of Grauman's Chinese Theatre, there with the crowds and the people in their fancy clothes and the noise and the lights. We stood looking at the stars' signatures and their footprints in the sidewalk.

Wow! We were really here. Wait till I told Judy about this.

Except that Judy was probably thinking and caring only about Kevin.

"Look!" I said, pointing to one set of footprints. "Carole Lombard! My dad's favorite."

"Never heard of her," Nick answered.

"Oh, and look! Montgomery Clift! Wait till I tell Shelly."

"But look what I found!" Nick said. "I found it!"

I turned and looked where he was pointing, then crossed the sidewalk to him.

Judy Garland. Judy Garland's footprints. I took a

deep breath and very carefully and deliberately put my feet into her footsteps.

For a long moment I just stood there. "My mother stood here," I said out loud, but I think I was really talking to myself. "Right here."

"And your feet fit there, too," Nick said, smiling at me.

I sighed and stepped away. "Yeah," I said, "but they're still growing. I'm going to be cursed with Sültenfuss bear claws."

I almost fell over then as someone jostled me, and I turned to say something, but when I did, I saw something else—something much more interesting. A jewelry store. A jewelry store with earrings in the windows. Big, beautiful earrings. And a sign that said Ears Pierced, Five Dollars. Earrings Included.

Five dollars. I had five dollars. I had five dollars and no one to stop me.

"I'm doing it!" I said to Nick, making the decision right there on the spot. "I'm doing it," I said. "I'm having my ears pierced."

Nick shuddered. "That's barbaric."

"Come with me," I said. "Please!" I pointed to the earrings I wanted—ones that looked like little chandeliers. "I want those. Aren't they beautiful?"

Nick shook his head. "No. But if you're doing it, let's get it over with."

Together we went into the store.

I took out my five dollars and told the jeweler what I wanted. He seemed mostly bored, but when he had me sit down in the chair, he must have seen how nervous I was. He took some ice cubes out of a little chest and held them against my ears. "Nothing to worry about," he said. "Once they're numb, it takes just a second to pierce them."

I took a deep breath and tried to be brave. "I have a high threshold of pain," I said.

Suddenly, for some reason, I thought of Shelly.

I had hardly thought of her for days. Was she all right? Was her pain, her sciatica, all right? And then the next thought: Did it hurt a lot to have a baby? Would it kill you to have a baby?

No!

"Ready?" the man said. "Are you numb yet?"

He reached for a small pair of gold studlike earrings.

"No," I said. "I want the ones in the window. The ones that really dangle."

"Can't," he said. "Not yet. You've got to wear these gold studs for a month before you can wear wires. And the ones in the window are twenty bucks extra."

I sighed. "Okay," I said. "Go ahead."

Out of the corner of my eye, I could see him pick up his needle.

I closed my eyes just as Nick said, "This is a totally barbaric custom."

And the jeweler said, "Vanity, thy name is woman."

But it hardly hurt at all. I mean, I sort of felt it, but I was numb at the same time. I figured it must be a little like getting embalmed.

When it was over and the gold studs were in and we were outside on the street, I kept looking in shop windows, admiring myself. I also kept looking at people who passed, wondering if they were admiring my ears, too.

But hardly anyone seemed to notice. Not even Nick.

"Well," I said to him, and I twisted my head, so he couldn't help but see my ears. "Aren't you going to say anything?"

He looked at me. "I already did," he said. "It's a barbaric custom." He grinned. "But on you it looks good."

I grinned back.

Wow! A compliment. From Nick!

I noticed then that Nick had a business card in his hand.

"What's that?" I asked.

"Oh, nothing," Nick answered. "Just that that jeweler had some great wedding rings. Just in case. For Phil."

There was a long pause. Then he said, "I mean, if Phil marries my mom, she'll be your aunt, right?"

"Right," I said.

"And you'd be my cousin?" Nick said.

"Well," I said, "yeah. I guess. I mean, sort of."

Did I want to be his cousin? I mean, I'd rather be his . . . What? What would I rather be?

"But we wouldn't be related, right?" Nick went on, like he was thinking the same thing I was thinking. Whatever that was.

"No," I said. "We wouldn't be from the same bloodlines or anything. We'd be like total strangers who accidentally had relatives get married."

"Good!" Nick said with a big sigh. "Because . . ."

He stuck his hands in his pockets then, turning away and looking in a shop window, and he didn't finish his sentence.

I wasn't sure what he was thinking, but I suddenly knew what I was thinking—a good, sensible thought. "Marriage," I said firmly, "can really complicate things."

And it could. Look at what happened to my mom. Look at Dad and Shelly and that new baby.

I turned then and looked at myself in the shop window, too—looked at my ears for about the twentieth time.

Man, did I look great!

Nick and I walked up and down all the streets then, admiring the fancy people and the crowds. After a while we stopped and had a chili dog and a soda. For some weird reason, even though I was nervous and kept checking my watch so we wouldn't get back too late, still, I didn't want this night to end.

I wondered if Nick felt the same way.

I had a feeling, however, that being Nick, he'd never say so, although he sure didn't seem to be in a hurry, either.

Eventually, though, it was eleven-thirty. Our night out had to end.

Slowly we headed home, walking close to each

other but never touching. And neither of us saying much.

My ears were beginning to throb some, and I worried a little about what Dad would say. I mean, I knew Shelly would love it. I figured Uncle Phil probably wouldn't even notice. But Dad?

Oh, well. It was done. He couldn't undo it. And I wouldn't worry about it yet.

When we got back to the apartment, it was just a little before midnight. "We should have called," I said, softly.

"They're not home," Nick said. "I didn't see their car. And tomorrow—tomorrow we go to that Hillary Mitchell's place."

"Right," I said.

Hillary Mitchell. My mom's best friend.

Nick used his key and let us in—in, and up the stairs, and then he opened the door to the apartment.

Opened the door to see Rose and Phil. Rose and Phil, who were sitting on the couch facing the door, Rose looking like a volcano about to erupt.

Beside me, I could hear Nick suck in his breath.

"You're grounded till you're fifty!" Rose said, glaring at us both but speaking to Nick.

"Now, wait!" Nick said. "You're overreacting—"

"Make it sixty!" Rose said. "And I'm docking you two weeks' allowance."

"Mo-om!" Nick bellowed.

"You think this is fun for me?" Rose bellowed

back. "You go out on the town, and I get to be the witch. I don't want you to be some punk hoodlum juvenile delinquent, but I can't do my job as a parent if you don't do your job as a kid!"

"It wasn't his fault," I interjected. "I wanted—"

"No, no!" Nick said. "It was me. And I'm sorry, Mom, really. Just tell me what to do. I'll do anything."

"Just go to your room!" Rose said.

Nick sighed. Waited a minute. And went.

I held my breath. My turn.

I looked from Uncle Phil to Rose and back.

Phil wasn't looking at me. He was watching Rose, a small smile on his face, like he was proud of her.

"And you!" Rose said, pointing her finger at me. "I don't suppose your father gave you permission to get your ears pierced."

Well, at least she had noticed. "Uh, no," I said. "I mean, not uh, exactly."

"Just don't shave your legs!" Rose said. "He'll never let you visit again if I send you home all hairless and full of holes."

I heard Uncle Phil laugh, but when I turned to him, he had put on this very stern face.

I turned back to Rose. Now what? Nick was grounded. Without Nick as my guide, would I ever find out more about my mom? I had found out so much. Yet I didn't feel I was finished. I still didn't know her greatest achievement.

And tomorrow we were supposed to see Hillary Mitchell!

"And you're grounded, too!" Rose said.

"Me?" I said.

"You!" she said back.

And she got up and stalked off to her room.

Leaving me to wonder how I was ever going to find what I had come here to find.

CHAPTER

XVI

*T*he next morning Rose was as mad as the night before, maybe even madder.

She actually made me and Nick sit on folding chairs in her office, like two little kids in the principal's office, while she made out bills. She kept muttering things about preventing us from becoming juvenile delinquents, and how was she supposed to do her job as a mom and other things that we were clearly meant to hear.

I wanted to interrupt to tell her I had just a few days left, and please, couldn't I go? But I had a feeling she'd tear my head off.

The better one to ask would be Uncle Phil—if Rose ever let me up off my chair to go speak to him.

We were sitting there, both of us trying to look contrite, when there was this double ping-ping as a customer's car pulled in, and we looked up to see more trouble.

Sam Helburn. Sam with the *smile*. Sam with the Jag.

Well, at least it wasn't our trouble.

Rose got up and went out to greet him, and both Nick and I leaned forward in our chairs, straining to hear the conversation.

"Good morning!" Sam said.

"Maybe for you!" Rose answered.

"Uh-oh," Sam replied. "Something wrong?"

"Wrong?" Rose answered. "Let's just say you're lucky you deal with kids who are under anesthesia."

Sam smiled. "Even without anesthesia, I always tell my patients to relax. Isn't it time for a coffee break? There must be a place we can go for coffee and . . ."

Rose was shaking her head no.

I was thinking: Yes! Yes! Go with him! Then I can get Phil to let me go.

But obviously Rose didn't get my mental messages because she just said, "Oh, I couldn't."

"You couldn't?" Sam said. "Why not?"

"I'm sort of . . . involved," Rose answered.

"Sort of?" Sam said.

"Let's just say I'm involved, all right?" Rose said, sounding kind of annoyed.

From her weary tone of voice, though, I had a feeling she was tempted.

"Where I come from," Sam said quietly but still

loud enough for me to hear, "involvement calls for a substantial piece of jewelry."

"Oh, I don't wear much jewelry," Rose said.

"Okay," Sam said, "so you don't like jewelry. But you do like good music. Liszt is one of my favorites, too."

So that was what we were hearing on the radio. Uncle Phil said once that Rose's choice of music sounded like Minnie Mouse squeaking in the shower.

"My parents loved Liszt," Rose said. "They were Hungarian."

"Yes!" Sam said. "I thought you were. Hungarians are famous for their beautiful music, their beautiful women, their—"

Suddenly Uncle Phil was there, standing right beside them, like he had appeared out of nowhere.

"Why, Dr. Helburn!" he said. "What a surprise."

Phil leaned against the car. "In the last four days," he said in this very controlled tone of voice, and ticking things off on his fingers, "we changed your oil, relined your breaks, rotated your tires, balanced and aligned your front end, and flushed out the entire cooling system. I thought we wouldn't be seeing you for another five thousand miles."

"What can I say, Phil?" Sam said, and the smile he gave Phil was not at all the same one he gave Rose. "I always feel so welcome here."

Uh-oh.

"You are!" Rose said. "So why don't you come by tomorrow and we can check that left front blinker?"

"First thing," Sam said. "I look forward to it."

He got in the car and started backing out as Phil turned to Rose.

"We should really flush out that line of baloney he's got," Uncle Phil said angrily. He mimicked Sam's tone of voice: "'Hungarians are famous for their beautiful women.' Ha!"

"What's wrong with a little flattery?" Rose said. "What's wrong with a little appreciation?"

"Are you saying I don't appreciate you?" Phil said.

"I'm saying he asked me out for coffee, like a real date. When's the last time you did that?"

"What do you mean?" Phil said. "We have a date every night."

"That's not a *date!*" Rose said. "A date is when I don't cook!"

She stormed away from him and into the office. Nick and I both tried to look as if we hadn't heard a thing.

But I couldn't help hearing Phil's last remark. "Hey!" he yelled. "I do the dishes."

I think it was that last remark that made her let us go, just to get rid of us, maybe so she could really have it out with Phil.

But anyway, Nick asked her if we could leave, and I couldn't believe he had the nerve. I thought she'd murder him for even opening his mouth. But she said yes, she'd allow us to go to Hillary's place since it was so close by. She also warned us if we weren't back in an hour, she'd have our heads.

Nick assured her we'd definitely be back in an

hour, and we were out of there, both of us checking our watches, because there was no way I was going to be late returning.

I had a feeling Rose meant what she said—not that she'd have our heads but that we would be grounded, this time for good. Or else she just might put me on a plane early and send me home.

It took no more than five minutes till we were standing in front of Hillary's shop, under a sign that said Hillary Mitchell Unlimited. Apparel with an Attitude.

We went in to find this incredible shop, this room hung all around with the most exquisite clothes I've ever seen—dresses of deep, rich colors, embroidered and sequined. They weren't overdone, though, or sleazy-looking or anything. I couldn't tell if they were new dresses or antiques, but each one was like a work of art.

The woman sitting behind a sewing machine in back was almost as beautiful as the dresses. She had thick, long hair and makeup that made her eyes stand out, but again, not cheap or overdone. Just exotic-looking.

She looked up when we entered.

I didn't even wait. "Are you the Hillary Mitchell who went to school with Maggie Muldovan?" I asked.

"Maggie Muldovan?" she said. "You bet I am. How did you know her?"

"She's her daughter," Nick said kind of proudly,

like he had noticed how much people had liked her and he was proud of it, too.

Hillary got up and came across the room to me. "Of course you are!" she said, holding out her hands to me. "It's the eyes mostly, but the hair, too. It's hers! I always said I wanted to trade hair with her, but she said I'd have to throw in my cheekbones. And now she's gone. She'll never get to see you anymore and to see how well you've turned out!"

Suddenly she threw her arms around me. "Oh, you poor thing!" she said. "You poor thing."

Weird. She was crying.

I mean, it was sad. But it was like a lot of years ago.

I stood there stiffly for a minute, then pulled away. "It's okay," I said. "Really. I was a baby."

Hillary turned away and dabbed at her eyes. "Sorry," she said. "I've been taking all these seminars to get in touch with my feelings, and sometimes . . ."

She broke off like she was laughing at herself, but her face was streaked with tears, and she fumbled for a tissue, a tissue that Nick handed her from a box on the counter.

"Sometimes," she said, "it just gets out of hand." She took a breath, like she was getting control of herself.

"How did you find out where I was?" she asked.

"Peter," I said. "Peter Webb said—"

"Peter!" she said, and again tears welled up in her eyes.

Oh, no! She wasn't going to do this again, was she?

But she put up one hand, like she was telling me she was all right.

"I'm making such a scene here," she said. "It's just that this is such a surprise. It's wonderful to see you. Your mother would be very proud of you."

"Thank you," I said, backing away from her a little more. "Thank you very much."

I wondered, though, what my mom would think of her best friend now. Did my mom used to break into tears this easily?

I bet she didn't.

"I remember Maggie so clearly," Hillary said after she had blown her nose and wiped her face. "And your dad, too. We'd all pile into his 'fifty-four Ford pickup—Chuck the Truck, we called it—sky blue with red leather interior." She smiled at me. "Does he still drive it?"

"Uh, no," I said. "But sometimes he drives a hearse."

Hillary looked puzzled.

"He's an undertaker," Nick explained.

"You're kidding!" Hillary said. "Jeffrey Pommeroy's an undertaker?"

I stared at her.

"Jeffrey Pommeroy's an undertaker?" she said again. "I can't believe it."

I swallowed hard. "His name," I said quietly, "is Harry Sultenfuss."

"Oh," Hillary said, putting a hand to her mouth. "Oh."

"Who . . . who was Jeffrey Pommeroy?" I said. "What are you saying?"

Hillary was shaking her head. "Oh, honey," she said. "Oh, honey."

"What are you saying?" I said again, hearing my voice rising. "Are you telling me my mother had another husband?"

I kept staring at Hillary. My mother—my mother was married before she married my dad? And nobody had told me?

What else had she done? What other secrets had she kept?

And then my mind began racing, racing over all the things my dad had told me about my mother and him—all the things. And then I had an absolutely terrible thought: maybe . . .

But no, I couldn't think that!

"Oh, honey!" Hillary said. "Back then people did crazy things."

"They sure did!" I said, and suddenly I felt tears welling up in my eyes, then streaming down my face.

"They sure did!" I said. I turned to Nick, and I didn't care who saw the tears, not even him. "They got kicked out of school!" I said. "They married truck drivers! These are my mother's greatest achievements? I'm really glad I came all the way out here to find this out."

I turned and ran out of the store, not knowing where I was going. And not caring.

CHAPTER
XVII

I ran all the way home, even though I was so upset I could hardly see where I was going.

Nick raced after me, shouting, "Wait up! Wait up!"

But when I run, I can really run.

No way was I waiting.

We were practically back at the apartment when Nick finally caught up with me.

He took my arm. "Now, now . . . now, look," he said quietly, but he was so upset he was stammering. "Now, just because . . . because your mother was married before doesn't mean . . . it doesn't mean anything."

"Maybe not," I said, wiping my nose on my sleeve and not even caring if I looked like a pig or not. "But maybe it does. If nobody told me about this, maybe it means they're hiding something else, too."

"Like what?" Nick said.

I took a deep breath. Even hinting about sex was embarrassing, but I had to tell him—tell somebody. Tell him the terrible thought I had had before.

I stared down at the ground. "My dad only knew my mom two weeks when he proposed," I said. "And I was born about nine months later. So maybe— maybe this Jeffrey guy is my real father. Maybe my father *isn't* my father! Maybe I don't have a mother *or* a father!"

"Wow," Nick said real softly. "Oh, wow."

I looked up at him. "Look at me!" I said. "I've got the hair and eyes of a dead person! And look at my nose! Nobody in my family has a nose like this. I've noticed that about a million times. This could be the nose of a complete stranger. I came here to find my mother, and I found—"

I broke off, then started again. "I found—"

But I couldn't finish.

"Don't cry," Nick said. "Come on. That lady looked pretty flaky. Maybe she doesn't know what she's talking about. Maybe . . . I know! Maybe Phil knows something. At least you should talk to him before you get all worked up."

I looked up at him, and even though I was so upset I could hardly stand it, I felt myself almost smiling. *"Before* I get worked up?" I said. "So what do you think this is?"

"You know what?" Nick said. He put his face close to mine, very close, and with one finger wiped a tear from my nose. "You know what you said about your nose just now?" he said. "About it being a stranger's nose? Well, it's not. It's . . . it's yours, you know?"

His hand was still on my face, and he was so close.

I stared at him, almost cross-eyed we were so close.

I swear, I was so close I could have kissed him without moving an inch.

And why was I thinking about *kissing?*

I swallowed hard.

"Nick?" I said, backing away a little.

"Yeah?" he said.

"This has been a very confusing day."

But that was just the beginning of the confusion.

At dinner, when I asked Phil, he said he didn't know anything at all about my mother being married before. And I really trusted him not to lie to me.

Besides, he seemed so surprised, he couldn't have been lying unless he was as good an actor as she had been.

"I don't know, honey," he said, folding his arms on the table and leaning across to me. "Your mom and dad never told me anything. But sometimes married people have their own understanding about stuff. They don't want to involve anybody else."

"But *I'm* involved!" I said. "How could my dad let me visit here and find out like this?"

I swung around in my chair, reaching for the phone. "I'm going to call him and make him tell me everything. Don't worry!" I said, in answer to his very worried look. "I won't upset them. I'll do it in my own subtle way."

I dialed home, twisting my hair around my finger as I waited for someone to answer.

So how was I going to be subtle? There was no way. The best way was to just say it, right? Just *say* it, right out. Get it over with.

It took awhile for someone to answer, and I looked at my watch. There was a three-hour time difference between California and Pennsylvania, but it was only seven here, so ten there. They wouldn't be asleep yet.

After about seven rings, Dad finally answered.

"Hi, Dad!" I said.

And then I couldn't just blurt it out. I couldn't. Instead, I said, "I just called to say I'm having a really great time."

"Good girl!" Dad said. "Go watch them tape Johnny Carson."

I swallowed. "Actually," I said, now that he had given me my opening. "I want to see Jeffrey Pommeroy."

"Great!" Dad said. "Great."

"Dad?" I said. "Did you hear me? I want to see *Jeffrey Pommeroy.*"

"Is he some new rock star?" Dad said.

So Dad didn't know either? Or was he faking me?

"Totally groovy, huh?" Dad said.

"Totally," I answered.

"Ask him if he needs a good tuba player," Dad said.

"I will," I said, and even though I had hardly asked a direct question and even though this was hardly a direct answer, I did feel relieved—at least a little bit. I didn't think Dad would lie to me. I mean, he might have left some stuff out. But he wouldn't pretend not to know this, if he knew I knew it, would he?

"How's Shelly?" I asked then.

"Well," Dad said slowly, "basically good, but . . ."

"But?" I said. "But what?"

"But the doctor wants her to stay in bed and keep real quiet just to be—"

"Let me talk to her!" I said.

Oh, God, I prayed, let her be all right. Oh, don't let anything happen to Shelly!

"Hiya, kiddo!" Shelly said into the phone.

"Shelly," I said, "what's the matter? Tell me."

"Oh," Shelly said, "that doctor is such a nerd. He told me to lie down and watch soap operas. Other than that, I'm reading magazines and polishing my fingernails. Very boring."

"You need me," I said. "You're sick!"

"I'm not sick!" Shelly said. "I'm having a baby. And I need you to have a good vacation, and when you get home you can polish my toenails, because I can't see them from here. Okay?"

I took a deep breath. "Okay," I said. "Put Dad back on, okay?"

I could hear the phone switch hands, and then Dad said, "H. Sultenfuss here," very perky like.

"Dad!" I said. "Are you telling me the truth? Is Shelly really all right?"

"Vada," Dad said, "you know I'd never keep anything important from you."

You wouldn't? You really wouldn't? But what if you didn't know the important stuff? What if my mother never told you?

"Like Shelly said," Dad went on, "she's not sick. She's just having a baby."

Yeah. And people die having babies. I should know.

"Okay," I said. "Bye, Daddy. I love you."

I put down the phone.

This was all too much. Shelly was sick! I knew she was. Or else why would the doctor make her stay in bed?

And Dad—I can always tell when he's trying to sound too happy, too cheerful. He was worried, too, I could tell. He might not have been lying to me, but he was sure worried.

I turned around to face Phil—Phil and Nick and Rose who were all watching me like they thought I was going to detonate or something.

"Shelly's sick!" I said. "I've got to get to the bottom of this whole thing and get back there."

I looked at Rose. "Nothing can happen to Shelly, right?" I said. "I mean, that thing with my mom was like a once-in-a-lifetime fluke, right?"

"Right," Rose said. She came across the room and stood beside me, stroking my hair. "She'll be fine, baby," she said softly. "She'll be fine. And so will you."

Right.

Then why was my heart feeling like it was about to break?

CHAPTER XVIII

The next day Nick and I were sitting on a bench across the street from the apartment where my mother grew up. Rose had relented—maybe because I had only two more days here, maybe because she felt sad for me—and let us both off from being grounded. We were just sitting there, looking at the house, while I tried to work up the courage to go over there and probably be disappointed again. But if I found someone who had known my great-grandmother, that person might be able to tell me about my mom getting married—if she did get married—to Jeffrey Pommeroy.

Of course the better place to be would have been at Jeffrey Pommeroy's house, but there was just one Pommeroy in the book, and we had already looked him up and called him. His housekeeper said he was eighty-three years old, deaf, and partly blind.

So there we sat, looking at my mother's house. Sitting there, I tried a trick I had learned when I was a little kid. I closed my eyes, then opened them, closed and opened them.

"What are you doing?" Nick said.

I hadn't realized he was watching me. "Well," I said, feeling a little embarrassed, "this is where my mom grew up. When I close my eyes, I try to imagine her real clearly, and then, when I open them, I can still see her coming home from school, going out on a date, carrying in groceries for her grandmother."

Nick just smiled but didn't say anything.

"I know!" I said, jumping up. "I'm weird. Come on, let's go ask."

We ran across the street and climbed the steps. As I climbed, I ran my hand along the banister and couldn't help thinking: this is the banister she touched every day. And this—I reached for the door—this was the door she opened every day after school. And this . . .

The door suddenly swung open, and a grumpy-looking, squat old woman appeared. "Hey!" she said. "What are you kids doing?"

"We're looking for someone who used to live here," I said, backing up a little. "I mean, we're not looking *for* her, but maybe you know her?"

"Maggie Muldovan," Nick said.

The old woman shook her head. "She doesn't live here now."

"Well, we know that," I said, "but—"

"Then if you know it," she snapped, "get going. This is private property."

Nick and I turned and walked away.

I wasn't even really disappointed. I hadn't really expected any more. Or maybe I really didn't want to know any more. Maybe what I had found out yesterday was plenty.

I sighed. "Sometimes," I said, as we went back to our bench. "Sometimes I think I'll never find out the truth about my mother."

"I guess it's different when they're dead," Nick said. "My dad's probably still alive, so I don't think about him much."

"Where is he, anyway?" I asked, a little embarrassed that I hadn't thought about that before—that Nick was missing part of his family, too.

Nick shrugged. "Eleven years ago he was working on a beautiful 1954 Austin-Healey. Great car. He took it out for a test drive, and he never came back."

"Never?" I said. "You mean your father lives somewhere in this world and you've never heard from him?"

"Not since that day," Nick said. "Not even a note. When I was a little kid, I used to think maybe he'd show up and surprise me on my birthday."

"Did he?" I asked, knowing from the way Nick was talking that he probably hadn't.

"Nope," Nick said. "Then I figured, it's probably easy to forget a birthday. But how do you forget Christmas? It's advertised."

I sighed and looked away. "I guess my father's going to be a mystery, too. My mother *and* my father."

"Don't give up, Vada," he said. "Maybe . . ."

"Maybe what?" I said, turning to him. "The only Jeffrey Pommeroy in the phone book is eighty-three years old, and in one more day I'll be flying back home. I've run out of time. I've run out of ideas. And maybe I should never have started this whole thing at all. Maybe it's better your way. Maybe it's better *not* to know. Not to know anything at all."

"Do you mean that?" Nick said.

I took a deep breath.

"No," I said.

I looked up as a police car drove slowly past us. Then I looked over at the apartment house.

I wondered if the old woman had called the police because we were trespassing.

But the squad car kept going. I noticed that Nick was watching it, too, as it turned the corner.

"What if . . . ?" Nick said.

Then he looked at me, shaking his head. "I mean, I can't believe I'm suggesting this. I mean, all I wanted was a lousy five bucks toward my minibike and . . ."

He jumped up and took my hand.

"Come on," he said. "It's our last chance."

Before I knew it, we were back at the police station, back at Daryl Tanaka's desk—Daryl, who looked very surprised to see us but not as annoyed as I would have expected.

This time I didn't blabber, just got right to the

point, because Nick was right: this was our last chance.

"Look," I said. "I really need to find someone. His name is Jeffrey Pommeroy and he used to drive a 'fifty-four Ford pickup, sky blue with red leather interior."

Daryl folded his arms and stared at me.

"Please!" I said. "Please?"

He shook his head. "Sorry," he said. "I'm not authorized to trace licenses for civilians."

"Give us a break, man," Nick said. "All you got to do is make a call."

Daryl turned to me. "I thought I told you to lose this guy," he said, like Nick wasn't even there.

"Sergeant," Nick said, putting on a voice that I hardly recognized—very meek and humble sounding. "Sergeant," he said. "I know I said some stuff last time that—"

"I think the phrase was sleazoid geek," Daryl interrupted.

Nick took a deep breath. "I'm sorry, all right? But we're desperate! We've got to find this guy because he knew Vada's mother and maybe he can tell her stuff that nobody else knows, and Vada came all the way out here from Pennsylvania and she's got to be back Sunday and . . ."

Daryl just kept right on shaking his head. "You're still asking me to break the law," he said. "Besides, even if I wanted to, I can't do it without a criminal charge."

147

"So charge him with something!" Nick said. "Who's going to know?"

"I will!" Daryl answered.

He and Nick just glared at each other.

This was getting us nowhere. Daryl was mad and Nick was mad, and I needed that address! Desperately. Because this *was* our last chance.

I took a deep breath then, and I actually surprised myself with what came out. I mean, I couldn't believe I was saying this—and to a police officer, too. "I'm not asking you to break the law," I said. "I'm just asking you to stand up with Maggie like you wanted to."

No response, not even a look.

I sighed. "But," I added, standing up like I was ready to leave, "I guess you're going to be a hall monitor your whole life."

I said the words "hall monitor" as mean as I could.

There was a minute's silence, a long, long minute when I thought we had lost.

Then Daryl was speaking into the phone, something about an address for Jeffrey Pommeroy and about this guy "going after the governor," and next thing I knew, he was writing something on a slip of paper that he shoved across the desk to me. It said: Jeffrey Martin Pommeroy, 21781 Topanga Canyon Road, Topanga, California.

I read it, then looked up at him. I had to smile then, not only because I was happy to have this address, but because Daryl was smiling, too—not a big, wide smile but definitely a smile. From the look on his face, I had the feeling that he felt very, very good.

"Thanks," I said to him. "Thanks a lot."

Then Nick and I were back on the street, with me holding the most important slip of paper I'd ever held in my life. Ever, in my whole, entire life.

CHAPTER

XIX

*I*t was the next day, and I was driving down the freeway with Uncle Phil, wearing the most beautiful dress I have ever worn in my life, on my way to meet Jeffrey Pommeroy.

Maybe.

We had had a big discussion about it the night before, Phil and Nick and Rose and me, about how I wanted to talk to this Jeffrey person, wanted to see him face-to-face, but I also didn't. I could just picture me going out to his house and then, the minute I got there, changing my mind and chickening out without ever talking to him. It was Uncle Phil who said not to worry. He'd drive me out there, and if I couldn't go through with it, if I couldn't go up and knock on the door, then Uncle Phil would just turn around and drive me back home.

But Rose said I had to have a new dress to do it in. She said a woman should feel her best when facing up to something like this, and that meant a new dress.

So together we went out and got one. Rose bought it for me, the most beautiful dress anyone has ever had—a deep bluish lavender with touches of rose and tiny beads and embroidery. It was one of Hillary's designs.

Then Rose had helped me do my hair. She had taken it out of the ponytail and combed and curled it.

When I came into the living room all dressed to go, I saw Nick actually blink, then blink again, like he was trying to be sure it was me.

He didn't say anything, not a single word, but from the way he was looking at me, I knew he liked the way I looked.

It was Uncle Phil and Rose who kept telling me I looked beautiful.

Funny, but a pretty dress did help.

So now Phil and I were exiting from the highway at Topanga Canyon, and I could feel my heart racing. I was glad I had put on extra deodorant.

"You're awfully quiet," Phil said.

I nodded. "Do you think I should tell Dad about Jeffrey Pommeroy?" I asked.

Phil seemed to think that over. "I don't know," he said. "He's got a lot on his mind now. Maybe someday—when the time is right?"

"Maybe," I said.

"But then again," Phil said. "Your dad has his own memories, and now he's got his own life. In a way, this could be a secret that you've got with your mother."

I nodded. A secret. I liked that.

I think.

Uncle Phil turned onto a side street, and I saw the sign: Topanga Canyon Road. It was a quiet, rural road, not suburbs like back home, but more like country, mountain country or something.

Uncle Phil drove slowly, looking at house numbers, then came to a stop in front of a house, well, more like a log cabin, with a brook in front and a little bridge that crossed over it. Number 21781 it said on the mailbox. Pommeroy, it said on the truck parked on the gravel drive.

I swallowed hard. Could I really go through with this?

I sat there looking at it. A log cabin at the foot of the mountains. A pretty, pretty garden. A dog on the porch.

This could have been my house, I thought. That could have been my dog.

Uncle Phil turned off the ignition and looked at me.

I wiped some sweat from my upper lip. "I came this far," I said. "I should at least knock on the door. Right?"

"Do you want me to come with you?" Uncle Phil said.

I shook my head no. "He might not even be home. And I should do this myself."

Uncle Phil nodded toward the little bridge by the stream. "Take your time," he said. "I'll wait there."

We both got out of the car, Phil on his side, me on mine. I waited till Phil went over to the bridge and stood there, looking down at the stream.

Then I took a deep breath, and without giving myself one more moment to change my mind, I walked right up the steps to the house, onto the porch, past the dog, who rolled over and yawned, and I rang the bell.

And then I actually said a prayer that no one would be home.

Someone was, though. After just a minute, a man came to the door, a kind of nice-looking, tallish man with thick reddish gray hair.

"Are you Jeffrey Pommeroy?" I asked in a rush.

"I sure am," he said, smiling. "Who are you?"

"I'm Vada Margaret Sultenfuss. My mother was . . ."

Jeffrey Pommeroy held the door wide open, this huge smile on his face. "Maggie!" he said. "You're Maggie's little girl. I was hoping I'd get to meet you. Can you come in for a minute?"

I nodded. "I'd like to. Thanks." And then I added, "You mean, you knew about me?"

"Who is it, honey?" someone called from another room, and a pretty, youngish blond woman came in from another room, followed by a small child, a little girl, hanging on to her mother's dress.

Jeffrey turned to her. "It's Maggie's daughter, Vada. Vada, this is my wife, Emily, and this is my daughter, Katie."

Emily gave me a big smile, and then she said, "Katie, why don't we let Daddy visit, okay?"

She and the little girl went back into the other room, leaving me to look around at this room. I really couldn't help but stare. The house was much smaller than my house, but it was so pretty! There were flowers and trees painted on the walls, and everything was so, so dramatic! The kind of room I wanted at home.

I thought again, This could have been my house.

We both sat down, Jeffrey on the couch, me on a chair facing him.

Did I look as nervous as I felt? Could he tell I was actually shaking?

But why? What was the big deal?

"I'm glad you're here," Jeffrey said, like he knew I was nervous and wanted to help.

"You are?" I said. I took a deep breath. "Your Katie looks a little like me when I was a little girl."

Jeffrey just smiled. "When your mother died, your dad got in touch with the theater company, and they called me. But I didn't think your dad needed me showing up at the funeral."

"You're probably right," I said.

Especially if my mother died having your baby.

"And then," Jeffrey went on, "I moved around some and got married again and eventually had kids.

154

I figured sooner or later our paths would cross, yours and mine."

"Looks like today's the day," I said.

"Looks that way," Jeffrey said, and he laughed.

Suddenly I was laughing, too. Like this wasn't so bad. And he seemed so friendly, like he wanted to talk to me.

Well, why wouldn't he? If I was his daughter?

"So how have you been?" Jeffrey asked after a minute's quiet.

"Well," I said, "I'm doing this report. . . ."

And then I burst out with the whole story, about the school project and coming out here to find out about my mom and then about Hillary Mitchell and how Hillary had told me about the pickup and about getting his number through the police.

Jeffrey burst out laughing at that, but I felt a little embarrassed.

He must have noticed, because he said, "I'm not laughing at you. It's just that listening to you was like listening to your mother. She told great stories, great, long stories with crazy accents and special effects—like turning the light switch on and off if she was talking about lightning. Audiences loved your mom. She was great."

"Well," I said. "I don't know much about her. I was hoping you could help me."

I took the paper bag out of my pocket and held it out to him. "Nobody else knows what this means."

He reached out and took it, and then he said, "Oh, jeez!" And for a long moment he didn't look up at me or anything. There was just this complete, utter silence.

I sat waiting.

He began talking then, slowly, dreamily, like he wasn't even talking to me, more like he was talking to himself. But the story he told gave me chills.

"We dreamed of working in the theater," he said. "So we drove to New York, to Broadway, where it was all happening. We wanted to get married in a French restaurant—don't ask why, but we did—but we were totally broke. So your mom found this little coffee shop instead that had some tables in the back with real tablecloths—that was important—and she got this minister who would work cheap, and he agreed to marry us there. But when we got to the place that day, it was closed with this sign on the door: Closed by the Board of Health. By then it had started snowing, so we got married right there, outside, in the snow. It was freezing. But wonderful. And then for our wedding feast, we had hot roasted chestnuts. And this is the bag they came in."

He looked up at me. "We didn't have a camera or anything, so she wrote the date on this bag and I remember her calling it our wedding album. She said, 'This will be a day we'll never forget.' And we never did."

He seemed so serious, so still in love, that I couldn't help it—I blurted out the question.

"Then why'd you get divorced?" I asked.

He sighed and shifted in his chair. "I could say we were just young," he answered "But that's no excuse.

You have to understand that Maggie was a pioneer woman. She could have led a wagon train over Pikes Peak and had fun doing it. She wasn't afraid of anything. But I was. I was afraid of a lot of things. And I guess I was afraid of her."

He was quiet for a time, and then he said, "Hold on."

He left the room and came back a moment later, carrying a tray with two glasses of lemonade.

He handed me a glass and sat down with his. "The French call this *citron pressé*," he said.

"Have you been to France?" I asked.

"Never made it there," he answered. "Or to Pikes Peak, either."

I sat drinking my lemonade, fighting this thought that kept creeping into my head: This could have been my home. He could have been my father.

Was he my father? I couldn't ask that, though, so I asked something else.

"Do you have any pictures of her?" I asked.

Jeffrey stood up. "I have something better," he said.

He walked over to a cabinet, opened it, and took out a huge film projector and a screen.

"Films?" I said. "You have films of my mother?"

He grinned at me. "Just you wait and see."

As he worked on threading the film in the projector, he said, "So what about you, Vada? What do you want to do with your life?"

"I want to be a poet," I said. "But do you know Alfred Beidermeyer?"

"I know who he is," he answered.

"Well," I said, "he said I should be a TV repairman."

Jeffrey laughed. "I guess they make a lot more money."

"It doesn't matter!" I said, almost feeling angry again. "I want to be a poet!"

Jeffrey looked over at me, a little smile on his face. "Maybe he was just testing you to see if you wanted it badly enough. That's what separates TV repairmen from poets, you know."

He began pulling down shades then and turning off lights.

"I haven't watched these in ages," he said. "The sound drops here and there. But you'll see your mother. We called ourselves the Appearing Nightly Players."

I didn't know if I wanted to see this, actually *see* her in action. I mean, I did but I didn't.

But now, whether I did or not, I was about to.

The first part of the film was hard to make out, with the camera zooming in on people crazily, showing a theater with a poster outside, then close-ups of people I didn't know, zigzagging all the time.

There was a dark-haired woman who was trying to shoo away the photographer. And then a blond woman, a woman walking toward a wardrobe rack, a woman who picked up a big flowered picture hat and put it on.

Someone yelled, "Hey, Mags, let's have a look."

At that, Mags—Maggie, my mother—turned to the camera.

"There she is!" I whispered.

She was wearing an old-fashioned lace dress, her hair full and flowing beneath the hat, her head tipped to one side, smiling this sweet, sweet smile. And she was beautiful.

She bowed to the camera, then spoke in this heavy accent. "Dahling, vere is my chauffeur? You don't vant I should valk to the stage, an actress of my overvelming talent."

I laughed out loud, watching her—hearing her! I didn't even know that home movies had sound all those years ago. And it was wonderful to actually hear her voice! This was my mother—my mother *talking* to me.

The camera jerked and moved some more and then was suddenly on a beach where everyone was playing volleyball and my mother made a great play.

And then we were back to a stage.

As I watched, I twisted my hair and tried to remind myself to stop. Rose had made my hair so pretty before I started out today.

Suddenly my mother looked right into the camera. "What if nobody claps?" she said.

"They have to clap!" someone answered her. "They got in free. Come on, act like a star."

Maggie started hamming it up for the camera, laughing and making faces, and I found I could hardly breathe, much less speak.

Here was my mother. My mother in real life. My mother *alive*.

And then I saw her do something—something that actually brought tears to my eyes: she was absent-mindedly twisting her hair around her finger.

"Next is our farewell party for Charlie," Jeffrey said to me, over the sounds of the movie.

The film focused in again on Maggie—my mother —and someone begging her to sing.

"I can't!" she was saying. "There's no piano."

"Please!" somebody begged. "Please, Miss Muldovan. I've crawled four hundred miles just to—"

Maggie smiled and took a deep breath.

And then she began to sing.

Why hadn't anyone told me my mother could sing?

I couldn't believe what she put into that song. Her voice was tender and powerful, all at the same time.

It was like magic, her voice. But then it got even better. It was as if really, in real life, right back then, she began to realize the true meaning of the song, and she put even more power and meaning into it—and I felt as if she was singing it directly to me.

Her daughter.

I could feel my eyes tear over.

This was her. This was really, really her.

My mother.

My mother, who would have loved me.

Her song went on, and I wanted it never to stop.

I needed to blink, to blink back tears, but I didn't want to miss even an instant, a blink, although my eyes were clouding over.

My mother smiled then, a sweet half smile, her eyes dreamy looking, as if she had something secret to smile about.

And then there was this slapping noise like the film was running out, and it was over. She was gone.

Jeffrey got up and turned on the lights.

"She had a beautiful voice," he said.

I nodded.

"Would you like to keep this movie?" he said, turning to me.

I swallowed. "More than anything in the world," I whispered.

Jeffrey finished winding it up, then put it in the gray metal can. "It was good to see Maggie again," he said, snapping the lid closed. "And good to meet you."

I looked down at the carpet. Could I bear to ask what I had come here to ask? And if I didn't, how would I ever know? Could I live with not knowing?

Maybe.

Maybe not.

But this I knew: I couldn't ask directly, so instead I said, "Didn't you ever wonder about me?"

"Well," Jeffrey said, "I mean, I didn't know about you till . . . till after she was gone."

"I thought you would've been curious to find out how I turned out," I said, still not looking up.

There was a minute's silence, and then he said, "Well, it looks like you turned out just fine."

I looked up. "Yes," I said. I knew I still wasn't being direct, but how did you ask this kind of question?

"I always knew I didn't have Daddy's nose," I blurted out. "His nose is particular. And I couldn't tell about my mother's nose from pictures. But now, when I see you and Katie—"

"Wait!" Jeffrey interrupted. He held up a hand. "Wait, wait, wait! Vada, do you think—do you think I'm your father?"

"Well," I said, "I mean . . . my mom married my dad after you. And then I was born . . . so I thought maybe you got divorced because of me."

Jeffrey smiled at me. "Honey," he said, "I would have been proud to be your father, but it just isn't true. I think I should tell you the real reason your mother and I split up. Come on," he said, nodding toward the porch. "Let's go out where it's light.

"The real reason?" Jeffrey said, as we stood on the porch. "She wanted to have a baby. And I didn't. I told you I was afraid of many things."

"Oh," I said.

"See," he said, leaning against the railing and looking out over his flowers. "Maggie had this vision. She said she felt she was going to die young, maybe because her parents did, maybe because—"

"She just knew," I said.

"Right," Jeffrey answered. "She just knew. And she didn't want to miss out on anything, especially motherhood. It got to be a real problem with us. I thought we had plenty of time, but she didn't. And she was right."

I felt embarrassed, but I let him go on.

"So," Jeffrey said, "I was even grateful when she found your father. Sure, I was sad. But she found someone who had the sense to love her the way she deserved. But most of all, I was glad she had you, the baby she always wanted. I know she died happy."

He looked over at me, then came and stood beside me, a hand on my shoulder. "And I wanted you to know that, too."

And then he hugged me, and even though he wasn't my father, or maybe especially because he wasn't my father—no, maybe especially because my mother had loved him—I hugged him back.

*B*ack at the garage, I spilled out the whole story to Phil and Nick and Rose.

Phil had heard much of it in the car on the way home, but I had to tell him again—all the little details, like about how my mother looked in the movies, and how she sang. And about that song.

The one she seemed to sing to me.

Well, actually, I didn't tell them the *whole* story because I wouldn't tell them I had been a total jerk and actually asked Jeffrey if he was my father— although later I told Nick, since he already knew what I'd been thinking. But I told them most of it and then held up the film to show them.

"I'm going to use it for my report," I said. "Jeffrey says audiences love special effects. My mother was really good at them."

"You'd better ace it," Nick said. "We sacrificed our whole vacation for it."

"Well," Rose said, coming to me and taking my face in both hands, like she did that first day I got here. "It's a heartwarming story with a happy ending. I'm so happy for you."

I was happy too, and so grateful to her for everything: the dress she'd bought me, her home, for lending me Nick even when he was grounded.

But I couldn't say all those things. So all I said was thank you.

I meant it, too.

We were all getting ready to go upstairs—Phil and Rose and Gomez were about to quit for the day in the garage—when there was the ping-ping of a car driving in, and we looked over to see—Sam.

Jeez! He came at the worst moments.

Now there'd be another fight between Rose and Phil, and my last night there would be spent in awkward silence with the music blaring.

Oh, well, their business, not mine.

I moved closer to Nick, who I could see was admiring my dress—or me in my dress.

"Sorry, Doc!" Phil called out. "We close for business at three on Saturday."

"Oh, this isn't business," Sam said as he got out of the car.

He turned to Rose, like Phil wasn't even there. "I just found this great little Hungarian restaurant that makes its own strudel, and I thought you'd enjoy the taste of the old country."

He bent and took a shopping bag out of the car.

"There's apple, cherry, and cheese," he said. "I think my favorite is—"

"That does it!" Phil said, or rather, he yelled it. "That does it! The strudel does it. I won't let some podiatrist with a Jaguar full of strudel come in here and—"

"Cardiologist!" Sam interrupted, his face suddenly turning red. "I'm a cardiologist, not a podiatrist."

"Whatever!" Phil said with a wave of his hand. "Look, Rose and I have sort of an . . . arrangement."

"What kind of arrangement?" Sam said.

"Yeah?" Rose said. "What kind of arrangement?" Uh-oh.

Nick and I exchanged looks.

"I'd be real interested to know what kind of arrangement this is," Rose said.

"You know exactly what it is!" Phil said. "Come on, Rose, what do you want from me?"

Rose just smiled at him. "Not anything you don't want to give me," she answered.

"You shouldn't settle for less than you deserve," Sam said.

"You stay out of this!" Phil yelled at him. "If I was the one who picked red with a black interior, I sure as anything wouldn't be handing out advice."

He turned back to Rose, his face as red as Sam's. "Look," he said, "this probably isn't the place to—"

She smiled. "Oh, this place is just fine," she said.

Phil looked around frantically, like he was cornered. "You know how I feel about you!" he said.

She nodded. "You think I'm a good cook. You like the way I fill out an invoice."

"Rose!" Phil said. "I'm crazy about you. I love you. I mean you and Nick and even this garage, you're my life. And even though you have lousy taste in music, you're the only woman who could look sexy in that smock. So what I guess I'm saying . . ."

He took a deep breath and looked around once more. "What I guess I'm saying," he said more quietly. "What I should have said long ago is . . . will you marry me?"

She grinned at him. "Do you really think I look sexy in a smock?"

"Does that mean yes?" Phil said.

Rose leaned over and kissed him.

And I mean *kissed* him.

And at that, Nick and I began to cheer, and even Gomez, who had stayed bent over inside a car through this whole thing, stuck his head up and cheered.

Sam just stood there with his strudel.

I almost felt sorry for him.

But not too much.

167

I had plenty of other things on my mind, like packing. Like getting stuff together to go home. Like trying to get things sorted out in my mind.

But this I knew: whatever I had found—it was all all right now.

It was all all right.

*T*he next day Phil drove to the airport with Rose in the front and Nick and me in the back.

Nick wasn't surly, but he was awfully quiet, and I had a feeling something was bugging him.

He stared out the window quietly for a long time, then stared at the back of his mother's head, then stared at me, and then out the window again.

We had left extra time to get to the airport, because I had an important stop to make and Uncle Phil had agreed to make it for me.

He pulled up on Fountain and Sunset and let me out of the car while they all waited, waited for me while I raced up the steps with a little box of cookies—those steps that would have killed me if I had to climb them every day.

I knocked on the door, but it was a long time before anyone answered, so I knocked again.

Had Mr. Beidermeyer been out on the street and I hadn't noticed him?

No, I surely would have seen him.

Again I knocked, and this time there was an answer. "I'm coming!" he yelled. "I'm coming, you uncivilized—"

When he opened the door, I could see he was surprised.

"I hope I'm not interrupting anything," I said.

"But you are," he said. "I was sitting down. And now I'm standing up. It's not as easy as it sounds."

I held out the box to him. "These are made with artificial sweetener," I said. "You said you're a borderline diabetic."

"You climbed those steps to satisfy my sweet tooth?" he asked.

I took a deep breath. "What you told me the other day," I said. "You know, that I should be a TV repairman—"

"Look!" he interrupted. "I don't pretend to be a guidance counselor."

"I know," I said. "You're a writer. You can't help it. And neither can I. And I know you weren't really trying to talk me out of it. You were just testing me."

He grinned at me, a slow smile that made his whole face light up. "Congratulations," he said. "You passed the test."

I smiled back, then felt kind of embarrassed or shy or something. "I should go," I said. "I'm sorry if—"

"Don't ever be sorry!" Mr. Beidermeyer said. "You'll waste your whole life apologizing."

"That's good advice," I said, moving backward to the door.

"Wait a minute," he said. "Since you passed the test, you should get a prize."

"Prize?" I said.

He went to the desk, picked up a piece of paper and handed it to me. "Maybe you can use this," he said. "Put it on your first book jacket. Nobody will know the difference."

I looked at it—his note from Dylan Thomas.

I would have loved to have it. But no.

"Thank you, Mr. Beidermeyer," I said, handing it back to him. "But I can't take this. It belongs to you. Besides, I know you'll get your book published someday."

"It's nice that you think so," he said gently.

And then I backed to the door and gave a dumb little wave, good-bye.

I made my way down the steps, remembering how I'd felt coming down here the other day. Was it just three or four days ago?

I felt much better now.

It took no time at all to get to the airport from there, and we all stood around saying good-bye.

Good-bye is always the worst part.

"Thanks for everything," I said to Uncle Phil. "You're the best."

"No," he said, hugging me. "You're the best. Now, don't talk to anyone on the plane and—"

"I already had this lecture," I said. "Dad's meeting me, and we're going to get some pizza and have dinner in bed with Shelly."

"Kiss them all, okay?" Phil said.

"I will," I said, and then I turned to Rose. "Goodbye, Aunt Rose!"

She hugged me back. "Bye, Niece Vada!" she said.

I moved away from her to where Nick was standing, off by himself, kind of moody again.

"I'm sorry you had to sacrifice your whole vacation," I said to him, half meaning it, half not, because I thought he had had at least a little fun.

I hoped he'd say so, too.

"Well," he said, "some sacrifices are worth it." And he moved with me toward the tunnel leading to the plane, as though he were going to get right on with me.

"So," I said, "it wasn't that terrible?"

"I wouldn't say it was terrible," he said. "It was kind of . . . of . . ."

"An adventure?" I suggested, smiling.

"Part adventure," he said, smiling back and walking all the way into the boarding tunnel with me. "Part miracle."

With that, he reached out and touched my cheek, his hand moving slowly along it.

And I did something I had never dreamed of doing—well, all right, I had dreamed of it. I reached up and put a hand on his face, too, running it along his cheek, his jawline, even over his eyebrows.

And then our faces just got closer and closer

172

together. Just like the other day, an inch apart. But this time I didn't pull back. He didn't pull back. And somehow, some way, we were kissing.

After a minute I pulled away and looked at him.

They were announcing my plane.

"Will you write me a poem?" he asked quietly.

"Ten poems!" I said.

Again they announced it—final boarding call.

I turned away from him, feeling tears fill my eyes.

Jeez! How many tears were there to shed on this trip?

But I would miss Nick. I would really, really miss him.

I raced down the runway, juggling my backpack.

I would miss him!

He was a pain. He was moody. He was grumpy.

He was wonderful!

I would miss him.

"Look in your backpack!" he called after me as I boarded the plane.

The minute I was on the plane and settled in my seat, I pulled open the backpack.

There on top was a small box.

I opened it. Inside were earrings—earrings! Those wonderful dangling chandelier earrings—the ones that cost twenty dollars.

And a note: "In memory of barbaric customs. Love, Nick."

Love?

I leaned back in my seat, wiping away the tears,

173

fingering the earrings. Remembering. Remembering
the kiss.

The kiss.

The *kiss*.

I smiled. Well, one thing was settled at least. I
knew now. I definitely knew: a good kiss beats a good
poem.

_____ CHAPTER

XXII

I slept a lot on the way home, and I dreamed, dreamed about all the good, all the bad, all the confusing stuff that makes up a world. And all the stuff that makes for growing up.

But like Maggie, like my mother, I didn't want to miss out on any of it.

And I couldn't wait to get home to Dad and Shelly and the baby.

When we finally landed and I had collected my suitcase, I made my way off the ramp—to find Arthur waiting to meet me.

Arthur! Not Dad!

"Arthur!" I said. "Where's my dad?"

"He took Shelly to the hospital," Arthur answered. He didn't sound real excited but more anxious.

"Is she okay?" I said.

175

"Well," Arthur answered, and this time he grinned, "she was making a lot of noise."

Oh, God, I prayed, oh, dear God, please let her be okay.

We raced to the parking lot.

And raced to the hospital.

Arthur had barely stopped the car before I was out—out and running into the hospital.

At the desk I slowed down just long enough to yell, "Where's Shelly Sultenfuss?"

I was already in the elevator, waiting, when the desk person looked up. "Third floor, room—"

I didn't wait for the rest. I just punched three and went.

It took forever for the elevator to get to the third floor. What was the matter with it? Was it dying of old age?

But finally, finally, it was there. The door opened, and I saw Dad at the far end of the hall—hair mussed, shirt hanging out, looking like *he* had had the baby.

"Daddy!" I yelled.

I flew down the hall to him, then threw my arms around him. "What happened to Shelly?" I said.

Dad hugged me, then held me away so he could see my face. "She just had a baby," he said, smiling. "That's all."

"We have a baby?" I said.

Dad smiled again, but even smiling he looked like

he'd been through a war. "A boy. You've got a new brother."

"Can I see him?" I said.

Dad turned and pointed to the room he had just come out of. "You're his sister!" Dad said. "You can do anything you want."

As I went into the room, I heard him call after me. "Hey! What's that on your ear?"

I tiptoed into the room—Shelly's room. Shelly was sitting up in bed, looking even worse than Dad.

But she was smiling just like him, smiling and holding this tiny, tiny thing, all wrapped up in a blanket.

I practically threw myself on the bed and on her, holding back just enough so that I didn't hurt her or the baby, and hugged her tight.

"Look!" Shelly whispered. "Look, Vada."

She turned back the edge of the blanket.

Tiny. My brother was so tiny!

"Look at his fingers," Shelly whispered.

"Oh, wow!" I breathed.

Dad came in behind me. "I'm sorry I couldn't meet you, honey," he said.

"Me, too," Shelly said. "But I had to push as fast as I could."

"Did it hurt a lot?" I asked.

She rolled her eyes. "You have no idea."

Suddenly there was this tiny sound, a mewing kind of sound, from the baby. Followed by a wail. And then a howl!

I had no idea something so small could make that kind of noise!

"Could I hold him?" I said, and I held out my arms, kind of tentatively.

But Shelly just handed him over, seeming happy to let him go for a minute.

"Maybe he's wet," she said over his screams.

"Maybe he's hungry," Dad said.

"He's okay," I said, jiggling him up and down a little. "You just have to sing to him."

I smiled at Shelly and she smiled back. I guess both of us were remembering the Supremes.

But when I started to sing to him, I didn't sing "Baby Love." I sang something different.

I wasn't sure of all the words because I'd only heard it once before, but it was the song my mother sang in the movie. To me.

I walked with him up and down the room, jiggling him a bit.

Slowly, little by little, he stopped crying. Just little shaky breaths, then little sighs. And then he was quiet. He really was.

I walked with him to the window, humming softly.

I kept him there by the window a moment, whispering to him, telling him about all the things that were out there—all the things I'd show him someday. I told him about poetry, and I told him about Nick and my first kiss, and about Uncle Phil and Aunt Rose—and that they'd surely come to see us this summer to meet him. And I told him about my mother, how she was this great actress and how she spoke in funny voices. I told him that she had a face for close-ups and feet like Judy Garland. And I told him that even though it sounded conceited—but he'd understand someday because he had a mother, too, a wonderful mother—that her greatest achievement was me.

About the Author

PATRICIA HERMES is the author of many highly acclaimed novels for children and young adults. Among her many awards are the California Young Reader Medal, the Pine Tree Book Award, and the Hawaii Nene Award. Her books have also been named IRA/CBC Children's Choices and Notable Children's Trade Books in the field of Social Studies. Her books have been praised for their "recognizable vitality" *(Kirkus Reviews)* and "rhythmic, homey text and genuine characters [that] resonate with authenticity" *(School Library Journal* starred review).

Minstrel Books publishes *Kevin Corbett Eats Flies; Heads, I Win;* and *I Hate Being Gifted.* Archway Paperbacks publishes *Be Still My Heart* and *My Girl.*

Born and educated in New York, Patricia Hermes has taught English at the high school and junior high level and has taught gifted and talented programs in the grade schools. She travels frequently throughout the country, speaking at schools and conferences, to students, teachers, educators, and parents.

The mother of five children, she lives and works in New England.

Point Romance

Anyone can hear the language of love.

Are you burning with passion, and aching with desire? Then these are the books for you! Point Romance brings you passion, romance, heartache, and most of all, *love* . . .

Saturday Night
Caroline B. Cooney

Summer Dreams, Winter Love
Mary Francis Shura

The Last Great Summer
Carol Stanley

Last Dance
Caroline B. Cooney

Cradle Snatcher
Alison Creaghan

Look out for:

New Year's Eve
Caroline B. Cooney

French Kiss
Robyn Turner

Kiss Me, Stupid
Alison Creaghan

Summer Nights
Caroline B. Cooney

Point Romance

Look out for the new Point Romance
mini series coming soon:

First Comes Love

by Jennifer Baker

Can their happiness last?

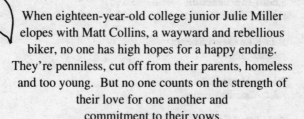

When eighteen-year-old college junior Julie Miller
elopes with Matt Collins, a wayward and rebellious
biker, no one has high hopes for a happy ending.
They're penniless, cut off from their parents, homeless
and too young. But no one counts on the strength of
their love for one another and
commitment to their vows.
Four novels, *To Have and To Hold, For Better or
Worse, In Sickness and in Health,* and *Till Death Us Do
Part,* follow Matt and Julie through their first
year of marriage.
Once the honeymoon is over, they have to deal with the
realities of life. Money worries, tensions, jealousies,
illness, accidents, and the most heartbreaking decision
of their lives.
Can their love survive?

Four novels to touch your heart...

P●INT CRiME

A murder has been committed . . . Whodunnit?
Was it the teacher, the schoolgirl, or the best friend? An
exciting new series of crime novels, with tortuous plots and
lots of suspects, designed to keep the reader guessing till
the very last page.

School for Death
Peter Beere

Avenging Angel
Shoot the Teacher
David Belbin

Baa Baa Dead Sheep
Jill Bennett

Driven to Death
Anne Cassidy

Overkill
Alane Ferguson

The Smoking Gun
Malcolm Rose

Look out for:

Final Cut
David Belbin

A Dramatic Death
Margaret Bingley

Kiss of Death
Peter Beere

Death Penalty
Dennis Hamley